Sem 8/14

The Selfish ~~Side~~ ~~Of~~ ~~Him~~ ~~Wanted~~ ~~To~~ Pursue This Attraction He Felt For Her.

She was smart and driven and damned sexy. His gut told him they would be good together.

Pierce wanted to go upstairs and hover. But suddenly it was important to make her believe that he was in control. That he wasn't an emotional mess. He didn't need her pity. Though, in truth, he was pretty sure she knew how close to the edge he was. He'd tried getting up each morning and pretending his life was normal, but that was a huge lie.

Distracting himself by flirting with Nikki might work for a moment. And contemplating the escape of sexual oblivion was tempting. But she deserved better, and until he could make sense of his screwed-up life, he'd do the honorable thing and leave her alone.

* * *

A Wolff at Heart
is part of The Men of Wolff Mountain series:

Wealthy, mysterious and sexy...
they'll do anything for the women they love

* * *

If you're on Twitter,
tell us what you think of Harlequin Desire!
#harlequindesire

Dear Reader,

My husband and I have spent many happy hours in the Blue Ridge, whether hiking or touring by car or photographing the panoramic beauty of these old mountains.

As I wrap up the saga of the Wolff family, I feel a pang of regret in leaving behind Wolff Castle, all of the Wolff clan and the timeless beauty of some of the world's oldest peaks.

After a Christmas book this December and a Texas Cattleman's Club book in January 2014, I will begin a new series called the Kavanaughs of Silver Glen. I am already getting excited about the heroes and heroines to come, and I hope you will join me in this new adventure.

Remember to visit my website at www.janicemaynard.com and also to join me at www.facebook.com/JaniceMaynardReaderPage. As always, you can email me at JESM13@aol.com. And I truly appreciate reader reviews on Amazon.

Happy Reading,

Janice Maynard

A WOLFF AT HEART

—

JANICE MAYNARD

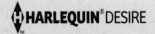

If you purchased this book without a cover you should be aware
that this book is stolen property. It was reported as "unsold and
destroyed" to the publisher, and neither the author nor the
publisher has received any payment for this "stripped book."

Recycling programs
for this product may
not exist in your area.

ISBN-13: 978-0-373-73273-9

A WOLFF AT HEART

Copyright © 2013 by Janice Maynard

All rights reserved. Except for use in any review, the reproduction
or utilization of this work in whole or in part in any form by any
electronic, mechanical or other means, now known or hereafter
invented, including xerography, photocopying and recording, or in
any information storage or retrieval system, is forbidden without
the written permission of the publisher, Harlequin Enterprises Limited,
225 Duncan Mill Road, Don Mills, Ontario M3B 3K9, Canada.

This is a work of fiction. Names, characters, places and incidents are
either the product of the author's imagination or are used fictitiously, and
any resemblance to actual persons, living or dead, business establishments,
events or locales is entirely coincidental.

This edition published by arrangement with Harlequin Books S.A.

For questions and comments about the quality of this book, please contact us
at CustomerService@Harlequin.com.

® and TM are trademarks of Harlequin Enterprises Limited or its corporate
affiliates. Trademarks indicated with ® are registered in the United States Patent
and Trademark Office, the Canadian Trade Marks Office and in other countries.

Printed in U.S.A.

HARLEQUIN®
™ www.Harlequin.com

JANICE MAYNARD

came to writing early in life. When her short story *The Princess and the Robbers* won a red ribbon in her third-grade school arts fair, Janice was hooked. She holds a B.A. from Emory and Henry College and an M.A. from East Tennessee State University. In 2002 Janice left a fifteen-year career as an elementary teacher to pursue writing full-time. Her first love is creating sexy, character-driven, contemporary romance. She has written for Kensington and NAL, and now is so very happy to also be part of the Harlequin Books family—a lifelong dream, by the way!

Janice and her husband live in beautiful east Tennessee in the shadow of the Great Smoky Mountains. She loves to travel and enjoys using those experiences as settings for books.

Hearing from readers is one of the best perks of the job! Visit her website, www.janicemaynard.com, or email her at JESM13@aol.com. And of course, don't forget Facebook and Twitter. Visit all the men of Wolff Mountain at www.wolffmountain.com.

For little Levi, the newest member of our clan...
We will always surround you with love.

One

Pierce Avery was having a very bad day. Such a bad day, in fact, that all other bad days in his life up until this very moment seemed positively benign in comparison. Stress churned in his stomach and tightened bands of steel around his head. His hands were clammy. He probably shouldn't even be driving, given his current state of mind.

Ordinarily, his first instinct during such a crisis would be to hit the river in his kayak. On a hot August afternoon, there was nothing like catching a face full of spray to court, paradoxically, both exhilaration and peace. He'd known since he was a preteen that he wasn't cut out for desk work. Mother Nature called him, seduced him, claimed him.

As a young man, his only option had been to find a career where he could act like a daredevil kid and get paid for it. Such occupations were few and far between, so he'd had to invent his own company. Now he spent his days leading groups of college kids, fish-out-of-water high-level executives or I'm-not-dead-yet senior citizens in exploring the great outdoors.

Biking, hiking, rappelling, caving and his favorite—

kayaking. He loved his job. He loved life. But today, the very foundations of who he was had crumbled beneath him like loose soil in a rainstorm.

He parallel parked on a quiet street in downtown Charlottesville. School hadn't begun yet at the University of Virginia, so the sidewalk cafés were only sporadically populated. Pierce's alma mater had shaped him despite his best efforts to rebel. He'd graduated with honors and a master's degree in business administration, but only because his father had pushed and prodded and insisted that Pierce live up to his potential.

Pierce owed his father everything. Now, years later, his father needed *him*. And Pierce couldn't help.

Locking the car with shaking hands, he stared at the unobtrusive office doorway in front of him. A pot of cheerful geraniums tucked against the brick building soaked up the sun. An engraved brass placard flanked a modern doorbell. The only odd note was a tiny For Rent sign propped on the inside of the window, backed by antique lace sheers. Anyone or anything could have been inside. A doctor, a CPA, an acupuncturist. Maybe even a massage therapist.

Charlottesville's thriving downtown community was rich with arts and crafts as well as more conventional businesses. One of Pierce's ex-girlfriends had a pottery studio just down the street. But today, none of that was on his radar. He barely even noticed the rich aroma of freshly baked bread from the shop next door.

Pierce had an appointment with Nicola Parrish. He rang the doorbell, knocked briefly and stepped across the threshold. In contrast to the blinding sunlight outside, the reception area was cool, dim and fragrant with the herbal scent of more potted plants in the bay window. An older woman looked up from her computer and smiled. "Mr. Avery?"

Pierce nodded jerkily. He was twenty minutes early, but

he'd been unable to make himself stay at home another second.

The receptionist smiled. "Have a seat. Ms. Parrish will be with you shortly."

It was exactly two minutes before his stated appointment time when the summons came. His handler nodded with another gentle smile. "She's ready for you. Go on in."

Pierce didn't know what to expect. His mother had set up this appointment. Pierce didn't want it. In fact, he'd give almost anything to walk out and never look back. But the memory of his mom's anguished eyes kept his feet moving forward.

The woman he had come to see stood, her hand extended. "Good afternoon, Mr. Avery. I'm Nicola Parrish. Pleased to meet you."

He shook her hand, noting the firm grip, the slender fingers, the soft skin. "Thank you for fitting me in so quickly."

"Your mother said it was urgent."

Unexpected grief constricted his throat. "It is. And it's not. In fact, I don't really know why I'm here. Or what you can do…"

She waved an arm. "Have a seat. We'll sort things out."

Her ash-blond hair was cut in a chin-length bob. Though it swung as she moved her head, he could swear that not a single strand dared to dance out of place. She was slender, but not skinny, tall, but still a few inches shy of his height.

He scanned the wall behind her head. Harvard Law. A second degree in forensic science. Various awards and accolades. Combined with the fashionable black suit she wore, he got the message. This woman was smart, dedicated and professional. Whether or not she was good at ferreting out information and answers remained to be seen.

Suddenly, she stood. "Perhaps we might be more comfortable over here." Not waiting to see if he would follow, she stepped from behind her desk and moved to a small sitting area. Now he could see that her legs were her best asset. They were the kind of legs that made teenage boys and grown men believe in a benevolent creator.

He sat down in an armchair that was more comfortable than it looked. The lawyer picked up a silver pot. "Coffee?"

"Please. Black. No sugar."

She poured his drink and handed it to him, their fingers brushing momentarily. Neither of her hands boasted a ring of any kind. Pierce drank half the cup in one gulp, wincing when his tongue protested the temperature of the liquid. A shot of whiskey might have been more in order.

The lawyer's eyes were kind, but watchful. She waited for him to speak, and when he didn't, she sighed. "The clock is ticking, Mr. Avery. I only have forty-five minutes today."

Pierce leaned forward, his head in his hands. "I don't know where to start." He felt defeated, helpless. Those emotions were so foreign to him that he was angry. Frustrated. Ready to snap.

"The only information I received from your mother was that you needed to investigate a possible case of hospital fraud from over three decades ago. I assume this has something to do with your birth?"

He sat back in his chair, his hands gripping the arms. His mother had contacted Nicola Parrish because one of his mom's good friends had worked with the lawyer in an adoption situation and had highly recommended her work ethic, in addition to her investigative experience. "It does."

"Are we talking about a situation where infants might have mistakenly gone home with the wrong parents?"

"It's not that simple." Perhaps he should have seen a shrink first. To sort out his chaotic feelings. Lawyers were trained to be observant, not to get into a guy's head. Although in truth, he didn't want anyone inside his head. Because if that happened, he would be unable to hide the dark river of confusion that swelled and crested in his veins.

"Mr. Avery?"

Inhaling sharply, he dug his fingernails into the thick, expensive upholstery. "My father is dying of kidney failure."

The flicker of sympathy in her blue-gray eyes seemed genuine. "I'm sorry."

"He needs a transplant. His time may run out while he's on the waiting list. So I decided I should be the one to do it. We ran all the tests, and…" He stopped short as the lump in his throat made speech impossible.

"And what?"

Pierce jumped to his feet, pacing the small space. He noted the expensive Oriental rug in pastel shades of pink and green. The buffed hardwood floors visible elsewhere. The fireplace that had been functional once upon a time, but now framed a large arrangement of forsythia.

"I'm not his son." He'd said those words in his head a hundred times in the last three days. Blurting them aloud made the truth no more palatable.

"You were adopted? And you didn't know?"

"My mother says that's not the case."

"An affair, then?"

Pierce winced inwardly. "I don't think that's a possibility. My mother is a one-man/one-woman kind of female. She adores my dad. For a moment I thought she might be lying to me about the adoption thing. But I saw her face when the doctor told us. She was devastated. This news was as shocking to her as it was to me."

"So then the only other explanation is that you were switched in the hospital nursery, right?"

"My mother's aunt, my great-aunt, was the doctor on duty that night. I highly doubt that she would have allowed such a mistake."

"So you need me to do what?"

He leaned his forearm on the mantel, staring at a painting of Thomas Jefferson hanging on the wall above the fireplace. The former president had fathered an undetermined number of children. People were debating his paternity even now.

Pierce had never once doubted his familial connections. He was as close to his parents as a son could be, though they'd had their differences during his adolescent years. The knowledge that he was not his father's blood son had shaken him to the core. If he wasn't Pierce Avery, then who was he?

"My mother is spending every waking minute at the hospital with my father. She hopes they will get him stabilized enough to go home. But even so, her focus is his well-being."

"And you?"

"I've informed my assistant manager that I may need some personal time. He's extremely competent. So I have no worries there. I'll make myself available to you as much as possible, but we need you to spearhead this investigation. We've told my father I'm not a match, but he doesn't know the whole truth. Clearly, this is very important to us. We need your help."

Nikki had never seen a man less likely to need help from a woman. Pierce Avery was big. Broad-shouldered, well over six feet and muscular on top of that. He looked like he could take a mountain apart with his bare hands...or scale one in a blizzard.

He was also the kind of man who instinctively protected women. She could see it in his stance. His sheer masculinity made something flutter in her belly. She was educated, independent. Financially stable. So why did the prospect of being coddled and sheltered by a big, strong man make her go weak in the knees with silly feminine arousal?

Those pesky prehistoric pheromones.

"It seems to me that our first step will be to subpoena hospital records," she said calmly. Pierce Avery wanted immediate action. That much was evident. So she would try to be accommodating.

Her would-be client grimaced. "The hospital was a private facility. In the mid-nineties, it was bought out by a corporate entity, absorbed and ultimately bulldozed."

"Nevertheless, the records had to be preserved somewhere."

"That's what we're hoping. How long will it take you to get them?"

Nikki frowned. "You seem to have the misguided notion that you are the only case I have to consider." His single-mindedness was understandable, but unacceptable.

"We can pay."

Nikki felt her hackles rise. "I don't like it when rich people throw their money around and expect everyone else to jump."

He glanced at her expensively framed diplomas. "Harvard isn't exactly cheap, Ms. Parrish. I doubt you've ever clipped coupons."

She willed her anger to subside, regulating her breathing until she could speak without inflection. "You'd be surprised."

He stared at her. "I've never cared much for lawyers."

One by one, he was pushing each of her buttons. Teeth clenched, she glared. "Are you always this obnoxious?" She stood, smoothing her skirt.

Pierce closed the small distance between them, running a hand through dark hair that was thick and a little shaggy. "Are you always this difficult?"

Their breath comingled. She could see a pulse beating in the side of his neck. His deep-brown eyes were too beautiful for a man. "I rarely brawl with my customers," she muttered. "What is it about you?"

He stepped back. It irked her that her reaction felt more like disappointment than relief. "I'm not myself," he said, looking somewhat abashed.

"Is that an apology?"

"I still don't like lawyers."

"You can't really afford to be choosy, can you?"

His eyes flashed. "This wasn't even my idea."

"No," she drawled. "Your mommy made you come." She taunted him deliberately, curious to see if he would tell her to go to hell.

Instead, he surprised her by laughing out loud, his entire face lighting with humor. "This is the first time in my life that I recall ever paying to be insulted."

She shook her head, bemused by the almost instant connection between them. A negative kind of rapport perhaps, but a definite *something*. "I do believe you bring out the worst in me."

"Bad can be good."

He said it with a straight face, but his eyes danced.

"I don't flirt with clients," she said firmly, shutting him down.

"Why is this office for rent?"

He shot the question beneath her defenses, leaving her gaping and struggling to find an ambiguous response. "Well, I…" Damn it. She was cool and deadly in a courtroom. But that was with hours of preparation. Today she felt quicksand beneath her feet.

Pierce cocked his head. "State secrets?"

She sighed. "Not at all. If you must know, I've sold my

practice. I have an offer to join a firm in northern Virginia, just outside D.C. With one of my law professors."

"I hear a *but* in there somewhere." His curious gaze belied his earlier gruffness.

"I asked for time to think about it. I've been out of school for six years. Never taken more than a long weekend for vacation. *Burnout* is such a clichéd word. But that's where I am."

"You must be pretty sure of your decision if you've already sold your practice."

"I'm not. Not at all. But even if I don't take the offer, I'm ready for something new. I'd like to work as legal counsel for a nonprofit."

"You can't get rich doing that."

"Have you ever heard the phrase *follow your bliss?* I want to live my bucket list as it comes…not wait until I'm old and half-dead."

"I can relate," he said, shoving his hands in his pockets.

She doubted it. He had silver spoon, heir-of-the-manor written all over him. She glanced at her watch. "We'll need to continue this later," she said. "I have another appointment."

"Doesn't matter," he said. "I've found out all I need to know. You can give me your whole attention. I like that."

Was it her ears, or did every word out of his mouth sound sexual? "I'm beginning a *va-ca-tion,*" she said slowly.

"Yes, I know. And some deep introspection. I can help you with that. Whatever your fees are, I'll pay them. And together we'll exhume the skeletons in my closet that honest to God, I'd rather not meet. But in the meantime, I'll help you become more of a human being and less of an uptight lady lawyer."

"I haven't said I'll take your case. And besides…what qualifies you to help me unwind?"

He adjusted the portrait over the fireplace until it hung perfectly straight. Then propped a hip on the corner of her very expensive desk. "You'll see, Ms. Nicola Parrish. You'll see."

Two

Pierce had been forced to cool his heels for six days before Nicola wrapped up her appointments and was officially off the clock. Even now, he'd been coerced into helping her move out of her office in exchange for a face-to-face meeting. Fortunately, his father was holding his own, but Pierce wasn't willing to wait much longer for the answers he needed.

At Nicola's request he'd brought a truck he and his dad used to transport inner tubes and kayaks. Pierce had to give it to her—she was a master negotiator. He could think of several hundred things he'd rather be doing on a hot summer day than moving boxes.

His mood, however, took a definite uphill swing when he knocked at the street door and Nicola let him in. She looked far more approachable today. A simple headband kept her pale-blond hair off flushed cheeks. Brief khaki shorts left those gorgeous legs on display, and the outline of her breasts in a close-fitting white T-shirt dried his mouth. The black espadrilles on her feet made her look far too young to be a successful lawyer.

He cleared his throat. "Truck's parked outside." His tone was gruffer than he had intended, but he was trying to hide his reaction to her casual attire.

Nicola frowned. "You're late."

Eyebrows raised, he promised himself not to take the bait. "There was an accident on the way over. I had to take a detour," he said mildly.

She swiped a finger across her forehead, grimacing. "It's hot as Hades in here. Someone got the dates wrong and turned off my power two days early."

"Bummer." He stepped inside, not surprised to see the reception area reduced to a large pile of boxes. "Do you live on the second floor?"

"Good Lord, no. That would be a terrible idea for a workaholic."

He followed her up the stairs, his gaze level with her curvy butt. "Most people who are workaholics don't admit it." It was a good thing he was about to do some literal heavy lifting, because he needed something to distract him from carnal thoughts about a woman he barely knew.

The room upstairs was just that, a fairly large open space with a tiny bathroom walled off in one corner. Clearly Nicola had used this level as a storage area, though in one corner there *was* a sofa and a table and lamp that indicated she might occasionally spend the night or at least catnap in the middle of a busy day.

She bent and picked up a medium-sized box, her gaze wry. "Self-deception is rarely productive. I know myself pretty well. Let's get moving. So far I've got fifty-three boxes ready."

His lips twitched. "Fifty-three? Not fifty-four or fifty-two?"

"Are you making fun of me?" She frowned, a tiny wrinkle appearing above the bridge of her perfectly classic nose.

He took the box out of her hands. "You finish packing and taping. I'll load the boxes, Ms. Parrish. I outweigh you by at least eighty pounds, and since I doubt you'd trust me enough to actually *fill* a box, this makes more sense."

She folded her arms across her waist. "You may as well call me Nikki. I think we've already damaged the lawyer/client relationship."

Adding a second box to his load, he tested the weight and decided he might even manage a third. "You call it damage, I call it progress. I'd just as soon not have a desk between us." *Unless you're sprawled on it and I'm leaning over you, licking your—*

He brought himself up short, grinding his teeth. Attraction in this situation was not going to help matters. "Nikki it is. And you can call me Pierce."

Nikki felt guilty. Not guilty enough to refuse Pierce Avery's help, though. She had fully intended to hire movers, at least a couple of college guys who needed cash. But when Pierce had called her office repeatedly for three days, she'd been frazzled and testy and had finally told him if he wanted a second appointment so damn badly, he could help her move her office.

She hadn't really expected him to agree. The ultimatum had been a toss-away comment, a reaction to his dogged insistence. Still, here they were. The guy with the big muscles handling her boxes with ease and the lady lawyer with the big brain reduced to panting over rippling biceps and the faint hint of aftershave that lingered in the stairwell.

Muttering beneath her breath, she finished up the last big pile of junk upstairs by stuffing it all into a trash bag and tossing the bulging plastic blob out the back window into a Dumpster in the alley.

With one last quick glance around the room to make

sure she hadn't missed anything of value, she descended the stairs, checking first to make sure Pierce was still out at the street. She didn't want to have to squeeze past him on the narrow stairs. Never had a man made such an impression on her. He was impossible to ignore, both by virtue of his forceful personality and his ruggedly masculine looks.

She'd dated wealthy guys in law school a time or two. But when all was said and done, each relationship ended by her choice. The gulf between her past experience and theirs was too great to sustain a long-term commitment. It occurred to her on reflection that it had been almost two years since her last date here in Charlottesville, and even longer than that since she had been intimate with a man.

Her wide circle of friends kept her social calendar filled, and on the rare occasions when she had free time, she used the extra hours to power through the backlog of work that always dogged her.

She loved her job. The diplomas on the wall were more than mere window dressing. They were a testament to how far she had come. Those same diplomas now rested back-to-back in a sturdy cardboard carton that would go straight into her car when she and Pierce were finished. The only real challenge remaining was her desk. She snagged two packing boxes, pulled up the appropriate spreadsheet on her computer to label them and started opening drawers.

Pierce stood in the doorway, unnoticed, and studied the woman who was going to help him make sense of the unbelievable. She worked quickly and methodically, using Ziploc bags to corral paper clips, pens, rubber bands and a host of other office necessities. He knew what she was doing. He'd carried out enough boxes to realize that she had color-coded and cross-referenced each one. He had to admire such single-minded organization, but he didn't possess any of those genes. If it had been left up to him, he would have managed to box up the whole place in half a day.

But Nikki Parrish was too meticulous to cut corners. Which was why she would never be searching for a wash-cloth and towel at one in the morning, as Pierce had been the night he'd moved into his new house.

While he watched in silence, he saw her reach into the back of the flat center drawer and extract something small that looked, from this distance, like a metal animal.

"Gift from an old boyfriend?" he asked, entering the room and sprawling onto her settee with a groan of relief. The window beside the fireplace was open, letting in a much-needed breeze.

Nikki clutched the figurine to her chest, her eyes wary. "I'm not sentimental, Mr. Avery."

"I told you to call me Pierce. And if you're not sentimental, then why do you have that whatever-it-is hidden away in the bowels of your desk?"

It was a fair question, and a simple one. But Nikki seemed taken aback by his query. She shrugged, turning the object in her fingers, her expression pensive. "It's a pewter collie. Someone gave it to me when I was a child."

"So if you're not sentimental, why keep it?"

A shadow of something dark danced across her face. "It reminds me of a particularly bad day."

"I'd think you'd want to toss it, in that case."

She looked up at him, her gaze bleak. "Sometimes we have to remember the past, even when it hurts. Acknowl-edging our mistakes can help us make sure we never re-peat them."

The note in her voice disturbed him. What did Nicola Parrish have to regret? Surely nothing too terrible at her age. He thought about pressing for details, but decided it was not a smart idea. He couldn't take a chance of pissing her off. Not when he needed her help so badly.

He rolled his shoulders, feeling the pleasant strain of exertion. Despite the physical nature of his job, two hours of lifting heavy boxes tapped into a whole extra set of muscles. "The upstairs is clear," he said. "And the outer office minus the furniture. All we have left is whatever is in here."

"You're fast."

"No point in wasting time."

"I appreciate your help," she said, her manner a trifle stiff.

He shrugged. "It's a quid pro quo, remember? I'll take you to dinner tonight and you can tell me what you've uncovered so far."

She leaned forward to drop the dog into a box…hesitated…and at the last moment, tucked it into the pocket of her shorts. "Dinner isn't necessary."

"You've had a long day, longer still by the time we're done. It's the least I can do."

"I'm not dressed for dinner."

"Doesn't matter. I'll go home and get cleaned up while you do the same. There's a new place over on East Market I've been wanting to try." He paused. "Are we taking the boxes to your house? I'll be quicker unloading than loading. I took my time packing them in, but it's still going to take two runs."

She shook her head. "My condo is tiny. I've rented a storage unit two blocks over. If you don't mind, I'll give you the key and the code, and by the time you get back, I should be finished. This desk and that furniture grouping go also… but none of the pieces in the outer office."

When she handed him the keys, her fingers brushed his palm. The two of them were close enough that he could inhale the not-unpleasant scent of overly warm feminine skin. He flashed for a moment to a vision of the both of them showering together. Holy hell. Not an auspicious time to get hard.

He backed away as casually as he could. She handed him a slip of paper with the address and the code. "Thank you for doing this."

Trying to ignore his baser instincts, he cleared his throat. "Have you had any luck with the records?"

She perched on the edge of her desk, one leg swinging. "You're lucky we live in the high-speed age, Mr. Impatient. Something came through on my laptop just a little while ago. I'll print out the attachments and bring them to dinner. With both of us looking at them, surely we can spot any anomalies."

His arousal faded as he once again felt the crushing burden of knowing that something terrible had happened when he was born. Did he really want the answers? No, but he didn't really have a choice.

"I won't be long," he said, striding from the room before she could read his unease. "See you in a few."

Unloading the truck was a piece of cake since he could carry boxes directly into the unit Nikki had rented. It occurred to him that she was literally storing away a large part of who she was while she tried to relax, unwind and decide the next step her life would take.

In that way, their situations were similar. Pierce, who had been comfortably assured that his life's course was mapped out, was suddenly faced with putting his assistant manager in charge of the business in order to wade through deep, unknown waters. He wasn't his father's son. Even now, with plenty of time to get used to the idea, he was incredulous.

As he drove back, he tried to imagine how he would react when he found out the truth of his birth. But the problem was, he had no idea how to spin that. No scenario made sense.

Nikki was waiting for him on the stoop when he got back, her face tilted toward the sun, stylish black sunglasses hiding her expression. He put the truck in Park and got out. "All done?"

She nodded, handing him a water bottle. "Yep. I feel a little sick to my stomach."

"How come?" He sat down beside her, their hips practically touching. Her arms and legs were pale in the afternoon sunlight. Workaholics were rarely suntanned.

"I hope I'm doing the right thing. I love it here in Charlottesville. But I keep thinking there's something more. Something I'm missing."

"Marriage and kids?"

She wrinkled her nose. "Doubtful. Kids require attention, and I'm not sure I can change my ways. I've worked flat out for all of my adult life."

"For what?"

"Validation. Fulfillment. Rent money. How about you?"

"My dad and I own and operate an outdoor adventure company. He pushed and prodded me until I finished a business degree, but that was merely a means to an end for me. I could never have stomached sitting at a desk all day. I'm an adrenaline junkie. More action. Fewer words."

Three

Nikki wondered if he meant that last bit to sound suggestive. Was he flirting, or was her overheated imagination reading subtext where there was none? It wasn't difficult to imagine Pierce practicing his philosophy of life in the bedroom.

She swallowed hard, envying him his casual confidence. She had worked incessantly since she was sixteen, terrified of the prospect of being broke and alone. Though she had found help along the way, much of her success could be attributed to sheer cussedness and an unwillingness to give up.

Her savings and retirement funds were sound. And even with this hiatus, her checkbook wouldn't suffer too much. But in her desperate push to achieve fiscal security, she had occasionally forgotten how to have fun. With big, sexy Pierce Avery sitting on her doorstep, literally, the prospect of playing hooky was suddenly irresistible.

His body was a thing of beauty, strong and muscular and perfectly proportioned. It came as no surprise to know that he spent his days outdoors in physical activity. He carried himself with the masculine grace of an athlete. Though he was a large man, he was neither clumsy nor inelegant. Sitting so close, she could study his hands—the long fingers, broad palms, neatly trimmed nails. It occurred to her that Pierce was the kind of man who could sweep a woman off her feet and carry her up a flight of stairs without effort.

When her breathing grew choppy, she knew she was in trouble. "I suppose we should get back to work," she said, wincing at the unmistakable wobble in her voice.

Pierce didn't seem to notice. He stood up in one fluid movement and held out a hand to help her to her feet. "I'm ready if you are." When his warm grasp engulfed her smaller hand, her knees trembled. *Wow.* This was a heck of a time to fall victim to an entirely inappropriate infatuation.

He released her at exactly the right moment, leaving her to wonder if all that dizzying attraction was on her side only. He held open the door and followed her into her office.

"I guess the desk needs to go on first, doesn't it?" she asked, trying to sound businesslike and professional instead of like a teenage girl with a crush on the star quarterback.

"It does," Pierce agreed, eyeing her dubiously. "I don't want to offend your womanly sensibilities, but wouldn't it be better if I call one of my buddies to help me with this?"

"I'm stronger than I look," she insisted. "I'll get this end and you take that one and walk backward. We can set it down in the doorway to catch our breath before we go the last bit to the truck."

It was clear he wanted to argue, but she was ready to be done with all this and go home. Now that the moment was actually at hand, she felt hot tears sting her eyes, despite her professed lack of sentimentality. This cozy suite of offices and the square footage upstairs had been a happy, comforting place—a spot where she had found her stride, cut her teeth, learned to trust in herself.

She watched as Pierce felt for a handhold at the corners nearest him. "Use your legs to lift," he said, "not your back. On my count. One, two, three…"

Just as she picked up her end, a small, furry rodent darted from its hitherto undisturbed hiding place, scrambled over her bare ankle—yuck—and disappeared into a gap where the baseboard met the wall.

She shrieked and dropped the desk, feeling an instant stab of pain when the unforgiving wood landed on her shoe.

"Holy hell." Pierce set down his end gently and lunged forward, lifting the desk to free Nikki. Her face twisted in a grimace of pain. He scooped her up in his arms and carried her to the settee, seating her with her legs across his lap. "Let me see how bad it is," he muttered. "Why in God's name did you drop the desk?"

Embarrassment colored her face a rosy red. "A mouse ran over my foot. I hate mice."

Her left foot had taken the hit. Gently, he untied the shoe and eased it off. They both sucked in a breath at the damage. If the heavy furniture had landed an inch to one side, it would have crushed several bones. As it was, it had caught the edge of her big toe, ripping skin and bloodying her foot.

He held her heel in his hand. "Do you have any first-aid supplies? Any ice?"

She shook her head. "I unplugged the mini fridge yesterday. My assistant wanted it for her college-aged daughter. And I've never kept any medicine here. I guess I should have."

He frowned. "I'll take you to the emergency room."

"No, please. Nothing's broken. You can see that. I'm sure it's not as bad as it looks. And it's not my right foot, so I'll be fine to drive."

Pierce had dealt with a fair number of sporting injuries

over the years. He was certified in CPR. In fact, he could be called upon to stitch up a life-threatening wound if no help was at hand and hospitals too far away. When he took groups into the wilderness, his responsibility was to care for them in every way.

But seeing Nikki in pain made him a little woozy. Her fair skin was so soft and beautiful it was a crime to see it damaged. Her feet were long and narrow with high arches. Only when she moved restlessly did he realize he was caressing the bottom of her injured foot with his thumb.

Immediately, he dropped her leg, and then felt like a jerk when she gasped softly. "I've got plenty of first-aid stuff at my house, and you could use a break with a change of scenery," he said. "No arguments."

"I was born to argue," she said, smiling at him despite her injury. "And besides…I have to be out of here by midnight or I have to fork over another month's rent. So thanks for your chivalry, but I'll be fine."

He knew she was an independent, successful woman, but her stubbornness at the moment frustrated him. "I know a couple of guys who owe me a favor. You can trust them with your belongings, I swear. I'll ask them to get the last few things out. Will that satisfy you?"

She gnawed her lip, clearly not used to letting someone else take the wheel. He understood self-reliance…hell, he even applauded it. But it was foolish not to accept help when help was at hand. Fortunately, Nikki must have come to the same conclusion. "Thank you," she said. "That would be wonderful."

He eased her legs to one side and stood up, situating her on the settee carefully. "Let me call and make sure they're available. Don't move."

Even though her foot throbbed like a bad toothache, Nikki didn't move. Not only because of her injury, but because she wanted to study Pierce while he wasn't looking at her. She'd been right about his ability to sweep a woman off her feet. He'd lifted her as if she were no heavier than a child. And she was not a lightweight.

It was in his nature to take over. She could see that. But he was genuinely making an effort to defer to her wishes. Which endeared him to her, despite his innate bossiness. She should never have made this lame bargain. Pierce was too handsome, too charismatic, too everything.

Her plan to take time off and decide on the next step in her life had to be a priority. Giving in to a moment's infatuation with a would-be client was impulsive and possibly foolish, neither of which normally described Nicola Parrish.

There was, however, some justification for her momentary lapse in judgment. Pierce Avery was the whole package: smart, funny, kind and strong. Heck, next to him a Boy Scout would look like an unmotivated slacker. Nevertheless, she'd do well to ignore the way her heart pitter-pattered when he touched her. The man was being solicitous, that's all. And he wanted something from her, so even his attentiveness was suspect.

Pierce needed her in his quest for answers. And she suspected that he was single-minded enough to take care of any obstacles in his way, including but not limited to playing doctor for his injured lawyer.

She flexed her ankle experimentally, sucking in a sharp breath when pain shot up her leg. Already her foot was swelling. And throbbing. Dang it to heck and back. This was a complication she didn't need.

Moodily, she watched her Galahad pace as he lined up replacements to finish her move. He looked far more relaxed today than he had when they'd first met in her office. An old, gray UVA football T-shirt clung to his broad, flat torso and exposed rippling arm muscles. His navy board shorts were well-worn, and when he bent over to pick up a pencil that had rolled out from under the desk, she glimpsed the waistband of his boxers.

More flustered than she cared to admit, she dragged her attention away from Pierce and decided to try standing up. She eased her good foot to the floor, swung her other leg around and gingerly stood, putting weight on her left leg. Not too bad. It was uncomfortable, sure, but with a couple of ibuprofen she'd be fine by morning.

Pierce ended his phone call and glared at her. "What do you think you're doing?"

"It's not a sprained ankle. I'm entirely capable of walking." Although the prospect of having him carry her again was temptingly sweet.

"The sidewalk outside is hot enough to melt steel. How do you plan on getting to the car?" He crossed his arms over his chest as if daring her to argue with him further.

"Well, I…" She trailed off, ruefully aware that she hadn't taken into account the actual logistics of *getting* to the car. As a kid, she'd had tough soles and could play outside with impunity. But that had been long ago, and Pierce had a point. Burning the bottom of her foot on top of her recent injury was not a pleasant prospect.

"Fine," she said, lifting her chin. "You may carry me."

Pierce smothered a grin. They were both sweating buckets, and though Nikki was trying hard not to snap at him, he could tell she was irritated, particularly since the job was not finished. She struck him as the kind of woman who liked her i's dotted and her t's crossed.

He managed a neutral expression. "In that case, let's go."

As he crossed the room in her direction, Nikki held up a hand. "Not so fast. We can't leave until your friends get here."

"They're going to swing by my place to get the keys. We'll lock the office and my truck and leave the truck on the street. I'll drive your car and take you home in it later. I can always get a cab."

She shifted from one foot to the other, obviously uncomfortable. "You've thought of everything, haven't you?"

"How can that be a bad thing?"

"I suppose I should be grateful."

"And yet you're not," he said wryly.

"Of course I am."

"But you'd much rather have finished the day on your own terms."

"Is there anything wrong with that?"

"No. But there's something to be said for going with the flow."

"I'd rather be digging a trench to redirect the flow the way I want it."

"At least you're honest."

"I need to go by my place first to get some clean clothes. Is that a problem?"

"Not at all, Your Highness," he said, swinging her up into his arms before she could protest. "Your wish is my command."

Pierce felt her slender arm curl around his neck and sighed inwardly. This was a heck of a time to feel unmistakable sexual attraction. He had a mystery to solve, and this woman was his only ally. He couldn't afford to let her know that she seriously did it for him. Everything from her silky hair to her classic cheekbones to her pinup-girl legs turned him on. With her in his arms, it was a short jump to imagining her in his bed…naked…calling out his name when he made her come.

Damn it. Lust was a messy complication. If he was smart,

he'd ignore her evocative scent and treat her like an asexual friend. Trouble was, there was nothing asexual about Nikki Parrish. She didn't flaunt her looks or really accentuate them in any way that he could tell, other than with a hint of mascara and some lip gloss. But her sexuality shone through, even when she was playing the uptight lawyer.

Pierce had to move the seat all the way back to get his legs into Nikki's small Sentra. She hadn't complained once when he locked her office door and deposited her in the passenger seat of her car. He started the engine and shot a sideways glance at his unusually silent passenger. "What's the matter?"

She shrugged, her gaze locked on the door they had recently exited. "I thought I was doing the right thing. Now I don't know. I didn't expect to feel so…"

"Sentimental?"

She punched his arm. "I was going to say conflicted."

"It's natural. Every turning point in life is an emotional hurdle."

"Wow. That's pretty deep."

"You mean for a non-cerebral guy like me?"

"Your words, not mine. Just because you didn't choose a desk job doesn't mean you're any less of an intellectual being."

"Sometimes I think it makes me *more* of a thinker," he admitted. "There's something about nature that strips away all the crap and reduces life to its most basic elements."

She gave him directions to her condo, which was only a couple of miles away. Again he carried her, though since her unit was on the ground floor, it wasn't far. Inside, he looked around with interest while Nikki collected what she would need.

Moments later, she came out of the bedroom. "I'd rather

shower here, if you don't mind. Can you entertain yourself for a few minutes?"

"Of course," he said, settling into a comfy armchair and picking up the remote. As he absently flipped channels, he studied her place. It was nicely furnished and tidy, but hardly big enough to toss a cat. The nearest bookshelf was filled with law books. No knickknacks and no pictures. Odd. Even her office had shown more signs of color. Though there'd been no photos there, either.

Nikki was true to her word. In no time at all she reappeared, wearing black slacks and a sleeveless white blouse. She looked cool and pristine, and he had a sudden urge to muss her up any way he could. "How's the foot?" he asked, noting her bare feet.

"It hurt like heck in the shower," she admitted. "But once we put some antibiotic ointment on it, I'm sure it will be fine. I did find some Band-Aids, but they're too small."

"I don't think you'll be comfortable going into a restaurant barefoot. And we need to bandage up that foot as soon as we can. There's a steak place out near me that does carryout. Sound okay to you? Or are you a vegetarian?" More and more people were these days.

But Nikki was already shaking her head. "I ate a lot of beans and macaroni and cheese growing up," she said, opening her purse and tucking a comb inside. "I love red meat. Any kind of meat, for that matter. So that sounds wonderful."

Her comment sparked curiosity, but he decided not to pursue it. For now, he was simply relieved that she was not going to fight him over his plans for the evening. "What about the hospital documents?" he asked.

"If I can access my email at your house, I'll print them out there. Is that okay?"

"Of course. Give me just a minute to order the food, and we'll go."

She told him her preferences, and after he placed an order, he moved to lift her again. She stopped him with a look. "The sun is getting low. I can tolerate the sidewalk. I appreciate the thought, but I'm walking to the car."

He put his hands high in the door frame, stretching his shoulders. "Did your parents ever call you stubborn?"

Her face went blank, wiped clean of every emotion. "No...they didn't," she said, her voice cool. "If you don't mind, I'd like to go. I'm starving."

He waited for her to lock the door and then followed her out to the car. Though it was hours yet until sunset, the sun's rays had tempered and a light breeze alleviated some of the heat. Nikki didn't say much. He wondered if he had somehow offended her.

The food was ready when he ran inside the restaurant. He paid for it quickly and jogged back to the car, oddly relieved to see Nikki and the car right where he had left them. He put the food in the trunk, except for one small sack. He slid into the driver's seat and handed Nikki his peace offering.

"What's this?" she asked, her mood suspicious.

"Hand-breaded onion rings. You said you were hungry."

Four

Nikki didn't know whether to laugh or cry. Here she was, at the end of an emotionally and physically draining day, on her way to have an intimate dinner at a man's house. And because she said she was starving, he'd bought her a snack in the meantime. As if humoring a fractious child.

When she opened the bag, the aroma of freshly cooked onions filled the car. She bit into one. "Oh, my…"

Pierce smirked. "I thought you'd like them."

She ate three without blinking and then, shamefaced, handed them over. "You'd better have some. I can't be held responsible if they all disappear. What are you? Some kind of mind reader? Onion rings are my weakness."

"So you do have some," he muttered, slamming on the brakes to keep from hitting a car that ran a stop sign.

"Some what?" She reached across the console and snagged a fourth piece of culinary heaven.

"Weaknesses."

She glared at him. "Of course I have weaknesses. What a dumb thing to say."

"Tell me," he demanded. "I want to hear one. Do you

occasionally forget to match your socks when you fold the laundry? Do you go eight months between dental cleanings instead of six? Is your checking account two pennies off?"

"Very funny." She reached for the onion rings again and he batted her hand away.

"The rest are mine," he said, shooting her a grin. "I worked hard today."

"So I've heard. Why do men always have to be rewarded?"

"Trust me, Nikki. Onion rings are far down on the list."

"If that was sexual innuendo, I'll ask you to refrain."

"Would I do that?"

"I have no idea. You're virtually a stranger to me."

"We've sweated together. That bonds people."

"Says who?"

"Everybody. Ask around."

She smiled at his bizarre logic, but didn't respond. They had left the city proper and were now traversing a county highway. Moments later, Pierce turned into a concrete driveway flanked on either side by massive oaks whose canopies met in the middle.

The property was lovely. Though they had traveled no more than five miles outside of town, the feeling of isolation and peace was remarkable. As the house came into view, she murmured a quiet exclamation. Pierce's home was constructed of mountain stone with a cedar-shake roof. Behind and to the side of the house she could see a pond. Horses grazed in a paddock to the right. Large windows gleamed opaque in the brilliant glare of the sun.

A well-kept, rolling lawn beckoned visitors to stroll into the nearby woods. Everywhere, shrubs and flowers bloomed. Slowly she opened her door and got out, ignoring Pierce's command for her to wait. He had followed a semicircular driveway and parked right at the front door.

Hobbling a few steps was no problem at all when the reward was climbing the stairs and looking out across a summer scene so idyllic it might have been painted by a Renaissance master. "It's lovely, Pierce," she said softly. "I don't know what I expected, but this is amazing."

"I'm glad you like it," he said simply. He had retrieved their dinner from the car and followed her up the stairs. After unlocking the door, he ushered her inside. Here she saw evidence of money in every tasteful touch. Oversized leather furniture. A massive stone fireplace. Oriental rugs that reflected masculine tones in the color palette. Artwork on the walls that probably cost more than her whole condo.

The floor plan was mostly open, with the kitchen leading off to the right behind a half wall. Pierce disappeared for a moment and then reappeared, carrying a glass of wine. "I put our food in the warming oven. If you can stand to wait, I'll jump in the shower and join you momentarily. There are rocking chairs on the front porch and out back as well." He handed her the glass. "Enjoy yourself. Relax. I won't be long."

She took him at his word and wandered out back, sipping the Bordeaux he had given her. Though she wasn't always a fan of red wine, this was lovely, smooth and fruity but not too sweet. Behind the house, the woods were kept at bay by another expanse of lawn, but here a fenced area was home to a family of basset hounds.

The dogs didn't bark at her presence, but they ambled toward her and stared dolefully, as if expecting to be entertained. Smiling, she tiptoed down the steps and onto the lush grass. Her foot still hurt, but she ignored it, concentrating instead on the beautiful animals. "Hey, there, sweet things. Are you Pierce's babies?" She bent and let them sniff her hand. "What pretty doggies you are." She crooned to them, talking nonsense. Her life, as it was, didn't have time for pets, but she loved them anyway.

Laughing at their antics, she squatted, wishing she could let them out, but unsure of the protocol. Suddenly, Pierce appeared at her side.

"You scared me," she said, rising and putting a hand to her chest. "That was fast."

"The guys just picked up your keys. They'll call me when it's done." He, too, was barefoot, his masculine feet oddly appealing. He had changed into dark jeans and a crisp cotton shirt in a madras plaid. "Say goodbye to the three stooges and come inside so I can patch up your foot."

"The three stooges?"

"Larry, Moe and Curly." He pointed to the dogs one by one and they set up a chorus of baying. "Later, boys," he promised. He took Nikki's arm, his fingers warm on her skin. "You could pick up bacteria in the yard. Let's head inside and clean you up."

"You're not going to let this go, are you?" It was a novelty to have someone so concerned for her well-being.

"Infections can be serious. You don't want to take a chance." In the guest bathroom down the hall he had set out a full complement of first-aid supplies. "Roll up your pant leg and hold your foot over the tub. I'm going to douse it with hydrogen peroxide. It may sting a little."

A little was an understatement. The antiseptic bubbled and fizzed, washing away any impurities, but the liquid hitting raw flesh was as painful as her shower had been. She bit her lip and closed her eyes until the worst was over. When she looked again, Pierce was kneeling at her feet.

He took her bare heel in his hand, and gooseflesh broke out all over her body. This was a terrible time to discover that her feet were erogenous zones. His touch was gentle but sure. First he dabbed the area dry with a paper towel.

Then he smeared a thin film of antibiotic cream everywhere the skin was ripped.

It wasn't exactly pleasant, but she was distracted by Pierce's closeness. She was practically leaning on his shoulder. If she was so inclined, she could ruffle his thick hair with her fingers. Feeling hot and shaky and breathless, she watched him wrap gauze around her foot and tape it with the neat precision of a trained medic.

At last he stood, his big body dwarfing hers in the cramped confines of the bathroom. "That should do the trick. At least you'll be able to wear a shoe over the bandage."

She backed up against the sink, feeling her pulse race. "Thank you. I'm sure it will be fine." He was staring at her mouth, and she wondered if she had onion ring residue stuck to her chin.

"Are you ready?"

Her abdomen tightened as little zings of excitement danced through her veins. "For what?"

A tiny smile tilted one corner of his mouth, as if he could see what she was thinking. "Dinner. Steak."

She swallowed, her mouth dry. "Oh, sure. Yes. Of course." She eased away from him and out into the hall. "Thanks for the medical attention."

"No problem."

In the kitchen, he insisted she park herself at the table while he dished up their steak, baked potatoes and Caesar salad onto attractive earthenware plates. Just as he sat down, she popped up. "We haven't printed out the hospital records."

He took her wrist and pulled her back into her seat. "We're not at a restaurant. We have all evening. You can do that while I'm cleaning up dinner. We can sit together on the sofa and spread everything on the coffee table."

"Okay." She subsided into her chair and cut into her steak. It was cooked perfectly, and they ate in silence for several minutes. Often she grabbed dinner on the fly or ate at her desk at home while she worked on case files. She had forgotten how pleasant it could be to share a meal with a man.

She debated her next question, but she wanted to know. "How is your father doing?"

Pierce froze, fork halfway to his mouth, before he set it down and took a long drink of his wine. "Stable," he said tersely. "I spent a couple of hours with him this morning. My mother hopes to be able to take him home in the next day or so."

"And then what?"

Pierce frowned, his gaze not on her, but on some unseen scenario that made him upset. "More waiting."

"When do you plan to tell him the truth?"

"When we know he's strong enough to handle it. And it would be a hell of a lot easier if I had more to say than 'The reason I'm not a match is because I'm not your son.' How do you tell a man that his only child isn't really his?"

"He's still your father. He raised you...loved you."

Pierce stabbed a bite of meat as if it deserved punishment. "I know all that. But blood ties go beyond simple reasoning. It's something primeval. I never realized how true that was until I had it torn away from me."

The conversation had taken a turn that curled Nikki's stomach. "Families are about love. When someone chooses to love you, you're connected, blood or no blood. Ask anyone who has adopted a child."

He looked stricken. "God, Nikki, I'm sorry. Were you adopted?"

The irony of the question tightened her throat. "No. No, I wasn't."

Pierce ate the last of his dinner and drank a second glass of wine while she finished her meal. He rolled the stem of his glass between his fingers, his expression grim. "If it was left up to me, we'd drop the whole thing. I don't need to pursue this."

"You say that now, but it would eat away at you. Some questions never go away."

His gaze sharpened. "Sounds like the voice of experience speaking."

She shrugged. "Lawyers see a lot of stuff people don't want to admit. Trust me, Pierce. You can't merely close your eyes and pretend this never happened. Sooner or later, you're going to want answers."

"Which is why I have you." He stood up abruptly, nearly knocking over his chair. "My office is upstairs. If you have trouble with email or the printer, let me know." He paused. "Do you need help walking?"

"No," she said. "I can manage without you."

Pierce rinsed the dishes and put them in the dishwasher, barely noticing what he was doing. In a few minutes, he was about to discover what might be an awful, terrible secret. If someone had asked him a few weeks ago, he would have said the only thing that scared him was the thought of his father dying. Now he had to acknowledge there were far worse scenarios.

The selfish part of him wanted to pursue this attraction he felt for Nikki Parrish. She was smart and driven and damned sexy. His gut told him they would be good together. But he needed Nikki's brain and skills more than he needed to sleep with her. At least for the moment.

He wanted to go upstairs and hover. But suddenly it was important to make her believe that he was in control. That he wasn't an emotional mess. He didn't need her pity. Though, in truth, he was pretty sure she knew how close to the edge he was. He'd tried getting up each morning and pretending his life was normal, but that was a huge lie.

Distracting himself by flirting with Nikki might work for a moment here and there, and contemplating the escape of sexual oblivion was tempting. But she deserved better, and until he could make sense of his screwed-up life, he should do the honorable thing and leave her alone.

Touching her could rapidly become an addiction. Even in a decidedly nonsexual situation like patching up her poor injured foot, he'd been hyperaware of her scent, her soft skin, her slender body. There was something so feminine about her. Which was funny, really, because she'd made it clear that she was strong and capable and didn't want to admit that a man could do things she couldn't…even if it was something as basic as lifting heavy furniture.

His head jerked up at the sound of her feet on the stairs. He met her at the bottom. "Well?"

She held up a sheaf of papers. "This is going to take a while."

Sighing, he held out a hand and motioned to the sofa. "Then let's get started. The sooner I know, the better." Suddenly, a thought struck him. "I'm paying you for your time," he said.

Nikki sat and fanned out four piles. "You helped me move, remember?"

"Our agreement was that I help you move and you give me an appointment."

Her smile hit him low in the belly. It was luminous, teasing.

She curled her right leg beneath her and sat gingerly, babying her hurt foot. "What if we call this a pro bono consultation? I've taken a personal interest in your case. And as of noon today, I am officially off the clock for six weeks."

"You don't owe me anything. We barely know each other."

"Well," she said slowly, her smile fading, "let's just say I'm fascinated by what you've told me. I love a good mystery, and I have a feeling this one is going to have more twists and turns than a Hitchcock movie."

"I'm glad my personal life entertains you."

She patted the seat beside her. "Quit sulking. The news might turn out to be better than you think."

"How can you say that? My dad is not my dad."

"That's not true. He *is* your dad. Being a father is so much more than dropping off sperm. He cared for you, spent time with you, showered you with love and affection. That's what a father does."

"You sound like a Hallmark card." He sat down beside her, preserving a careful distance.

"I hope you're not as cynical as you seem."

"I'm not cynical at all," he protested. Staring grimly at the pile of papers, he evaluated her impassioned definition of fatherhood. "I always had this notion that one day I'd produce a kid and he and my dad and I would do things together…you know…generation to generation."

"You still can. No matter what. Forget about genetics for a moment. You *love* your dad. And he's going to adore any baby that's yours." She patted his knee. "Give yourself time. I know the news was shocking, but I think you'll find that in the end your relationship with your dad is no different than it ever has been."

"I can't help him with the transplant." His throat swelled shut. His eyes stung. Though he stared blindly now, his eyes locked desperately on the stack of records, he could practically feel Nikki's compassionate gaze.

She sighed audibly. "That's true. But even if you *had* been his blood son, the markers might not have lined up.

As it is now, the most you can do for him and your mom is to get to the bottom of this."

"What if he doesn't make it? What if they don't find a donor?"

"You can't think like that. I know this is huge. I'm not minimizing what has happened to you. Truly, I'm not. But it's like having the breath knocked out of you when you're a kid. It feels like you're dying, and it's scary as hell. Sooner or later, though, your lungs start working again and you know you're going to be okay."

He straightened his spine, unaccountably encouraged by her sheer conviction. "You must be very good at your job." He shot her a sideways look and sat back, feeling a bit of his burden shift and lift. "Thank you, Nicola Parrish. You're a very nice woman."

Her cheeks turned pink. "I can be hard as nails when I have to be."

"And when is that?"

"Oh, you know…dealing with a deadbeat dad in court. Talking to a drug addict who's stealing to support a habit. Facing down a chauvinistic judge who thinks women need to be in the kitchen, not in front of the bench."

His eyebrows rose. "Is that still a problem…honestly?"

"Not often. But occasionally. And though you would think it's only the older ones close to retirement, sometimes it's a young man. Jerks transcend age and class. I met more than a few along the way in school."

"I'll bet you were one of those annoying people who ruined the curve for everyone else."

Her chin lifted. "I believe in doing a job one hundred percent or not at all."

"Which is why you're going to see this through."

"I told you, I love a mystery, a puzzle. And I never give up until I get the answers. But I have to warn you, I'll keep going to the end. Even if the truth is something you don't want to hear."

He clasped his hands behind his neck and leaned back into the sofa, feigning relaxation, though his guts were in a knot. "I'm scared," he drawled, only half kidding.

She uncurled her leg and sat up straight, both feet on the floor. "You don't have to be," she said, answering his attempt at humor with an adorably serious expression. "The truth may hurt when we're not expecting it, but secrets are far more deadly. Trust me, Pierce. You're doing the right thing."

Five

Nikki winced at Pierce's expression. She had no clue what he was thinking, but replaying her words in her head, she realized how she must sound to him. Insufferably sure of her own capabilities, and bossy to boot. It wasn't a great tack to take with a man. A truth that had been pointed out to her on more than one occasion. But if she had to hide who she was to be part of a relationship, she'd pass, *thank you very much*.

Not that she and Pierce were in a relationship, but still…

Pierce picked up a sheet of paper. "No use putting it off." He sounded more resigned than anything.

"Indeed." She opened her laptop and prepared a blank document.

"What's that for?" he asked.

"I like to make notes as we go along. Memory is a tricky thing. So I document things I either want to go back to later or that may turn out to be key points. Nothing formal at this stage. More like a running commentary."

"How do I know what I'm looking for?"

"You don't. Not really. You can check the basic facts, of

course. But if someone deliberately perpetrated fraud, I'm sure they will have tried to cover their tracks."

"Great," he muttered. "A needle in a haystack that's been buried for thirty-plus years. No problem."

She handed him roughly half of the pages she'd printed out. "Man up, Mr. Avery. All good detectives have to slog though the mud. For an outdoorsman, that should be right up your alley."

Pierce read automatically, though with less than perfect attention. He noted details like birth weight and time of delivery and length of newborn, all of which he had seen documented in his baby book in his mom's careful handwriting. Page by page, he scanned lines of medical jargon. There were sections about medicines administered, blood pressure recordings and body temps, both mom and baby.

Nothing jumped out at him.

After half an hour, Nikki handed him her stack. "Let's swap. Maybe I'll see something you missed, and vice versa."

The new pages were no more helpful. He found anecdotal descriptions of his mom's labor. According to the records, it had been normal in every way. But something suddenly struck him. "Why aren't there copies of ultrasounds? Seems like that should have been in here."

Nikki pursed her lips. "Good point. I'm friends with my ob-gyn. Let me give her a call. Maybe those records were stored separately in radiology."

As Pierce continued reading, Nikki disappeared for at least fifteen minutes. When she returned, her expression was wry. "Not to make you feel old or anything, but apparently back in the early eighties, ultrasounds were by no means routine. As a rule, they were used only in high-risk pregnancy situations, and sometimes not even then, because the technology was new and expensive and no one was one hundred percent sure they were safe."

Pierce was shocked. "Wow. I never thought of that. I assumed they had been around forever."

"Me, too."

"I can't imagine not seeing those little black-and-white pictures. I have friends who framed theirs."

"But now you know why they're not in your record."

Pierce sat up and rolled his neck. "This doesn't seem to be getting us anywhere," he said, feeling the muscles in his back kink and burn. "I wanted to take you out on a trail near here this evening, one that has a beautiful view. But not with your foot messed up. How about a drive? I need to get outside and breathe."

"You should go by yourself," Nikki said. "You deserve a break, and we've done enough for one day. But if you'll drop me at my place, I'd appreciate it."

"Trying to get away from me?" It annoyed him that even the thought of her leaving was unpleasant. He enjoyed his own company and the peace and quiet of his home at the end of a busy day. Yet with Nikki ensconced on his sofa, drinking his wine and smiling at him with those eyes that seemed to shift from blue to pewter and everything in between, he found himself needing her company more than was comfortable.

She nibbled her bottom lip, her thoughts hard to read on her face. "Not trying to get away," she said carefully. "But wanting not to outstay my welcome."

He tossed the records on the table and stood. "I'll let you know when that happens, I promise. Grab that afghan. I like the top down."

Perhaps it was bragging, but he couldn't wait to show her his 300 SL. He ushered her out to the garage, opening the double-wide doors to let her enter before him. Though he wasn't a total automotive freak, he did own seven vehicles of one kind or another, everything from a vintage Kawasaki motorcycle to a John Deere tractor he used for mowing. But he waited for her reaction to the one car that was his pride and joy.

Fortunately, Nikki was suitably impressed. "This is beyond cool," she breathed, sliding into the passenger seat and caressing the butter-soft burgundy leather.

Pierce averted his eyes from her sensual gesture and checked the gas gauge. "I thought you might like it. It's a 1960 Mercedes-Benz roadster. The cream paint and chrome are original. I bought it at auction when I was seventeen and spent the next five years rebuilding the engine and tracking down authentic parts. My dad and I worked on it summers and weekends."

Again, without meaning to, he had stumbled into painful territory. Nikki remained silent, no doubt picking up on his mental confusion. Each time he told her something about his dad, he couldn't escape the subtext. *His dad wasn't his dad.*

Jaw clenched, he came to a conclusion. He was tired of rehashing the same fruitless fact. For the rest of the day, he planned on enjoying Nikki's company and forgetting why they had met in the first place.

As he backed carefully out of the garage and swung around on the driveway, she frowned. "What kind of seventeen-year-old kid can buy a car like this?"

Pierce grinned as he pulled out onto the highway and picked up speed. "First of all, you have to understand that the engine had been ruined by someone putting a foreign substance into the gas tank. And secondly, the guy selling it didn't know what he had."

"So you took advantage of him."

Pierce shrugged. "I was a minor. He was a grown adult. I figured he ought to know better."

"And your parents allowed this?"

"Not exactly. I took money out of my college account without asking."

She half turned in her seat, a hand to the side of her head as the wind whipped her sunshine hair. "Oh, my gosh. I would have killed you."

He chuckled, this memory a lighthearted one. "They nearly did. Dad tried to return the car, but that was a no-go. The seller was adamant. So as punishment, I wasn't allowed to touch my new toy for an entire six months. And I had to make straight A's on my next report card."

"That shouldn't have been too hard. You seem like a pretty smart guy."

"I had undiagnosed ADHD. School was torture."

"But you told me you even have a master's degree."

"Only because my parents pushed and prodded me all along the way. Tutors, bribery and lots of TLC. I was damned lucky."

"Yes, you were."

Even an obtuse man couldn't have missed the irony in her voice. Pierce took the entrance ramp to Skyline Drive, north of the Blue Ridge Parkway, and settled into a safe speed. Given his druthers, he'd have pushed the car to its limits, but despite a few self-destructive tendencies in his adolescence, he now had a healthy respect for the laws of the land.

He glanced at his passenger. "We've talked way too much about me," he said, pulling his sunglasses from the visor as the late-evening sun threatened to blind him around one curve and another. "What about you? Where did you grow up?"

Out of the corner of his eye, he saw her wrap the thin mohair afghan more tightly around her shoulders. "Nowhere you've ever heard of—a tiny town in the Midwest. That's why I love these mountains so much."

"Do you still have family back there?"

"No."

His was a perfectly normal question. But between Nikki's body language and the tone of her voice, he got the message. *Not up for discussion.* On the one hand, he could choose to be irritated, because she knew so much about him and he knew next to nothing about her. But the fact that he had *asked* her to delve into his past gave her carte blanche to poke and prod. He had no reason or right to cross-examine *her,* particularly when it was so clear that she did not want to share.

Instead of allowing the uncomfortable moment to ruin the evening, he chose to brush it off. Hopefully, she would learn to trust him enough to share her secrets. She'd claimed that secrets were deadly. He wasn't so sure. Sometimes he was convinced that ignorance was bliss. And in his case, that adage might be truer than he wanted to admit.

Nikki was in heaven. The wind in her hair, the sun on her face. A fascinatingly complex, delightfully sexy man at her side. He wasn't *her* man. He was simply *a* man. But even lawyers didn't have to quibble over every nonessential detail. Today she was free. A woman without a job. That thought should have scared her, and it had on more than one sleepless night when she was contemplating how best to shape the next decade of her life. Did she really want to be a junior partner in a high-powered D.C. firm? Did she want the pressure, the scrutiny of being the new kid on the block?

The offer from her former professor was flattering, really flattering. And she had given it serious thought. It wasn't as if she would be walking away from a significant other in Charlottesville. She had many friends, but no one special in her life. No one who would be devastated if she left. So why couldn't she commit? Pick up the phone and make the call. Why was it necessary to create a false dead-line of six weeks? Was she really going to be any more equipped to make a decision then than now?

Closing out all of her cases and giving herself time for personal reflection had seemed like a good idea on paper. But truth be told, she probably would have been going nuts after a few days with nothing to do. Pierce's crisis couldn't have come at a better time. By throwing herself wholeheartedly into his problems, she could avoid her own.

His case was personal to her. So much of what he was experiencing hit her at a gut level. She knew the agony of not knowing, and she wanted to help. Spending time with him would be no hardship. His wit and banter were entertaining, and even if she had no plans to act on it, the sexual tension between the two of them was impossible to miss.

Again, she was flattered. But a more unlikely couple would be hard to find. Nikki liked her novels and her research tomes and her case files and her cozy condo. Nothing made her happier than to prowl through a bookstore or a library for hours at a time. Pierce enjoyed the challenge of man versus nature. He was a physically perfect specimen, a guy in his element when he was *in* the elements. Her inward joke made her smile.

Pierce probably enjoyed camping. She shuddered at the thought. Her idea of the perfect accommodations was a Hampton Inn with free breakfast. If she was lucky, she and Pierce would be so busy cracking the code of his messed-up lineage that they wouldn't have time for him to "help her unwind."

Thanks, but no thanks. She was as relaxed as she wanted or needed to be. Testing her physical prowess, even under the tutelage of a natural athlete, had all the appeal of a root canal without anesthesia.

She wasn't stupid. Anyone could see that Pierce was conflicted. Part of him knew he had to uncover the truth. But another part of him was inclined to grab any diversion, even if it meant teaching an uptight lawyer how to kick back. It would be up to Nikki to keep the investigation on track. If she let Pierce mold the agenda, they might end up doing something really dumb. Like fooling around and pretending it was more than it was.

Pierce needed to concentrate on what was important, and hormones were seldom important, in her opinion. He was dealing with some tough stuff, with more to come. Her own situation might be of some help to him later...when he was able process all of this. But for now, she saw no need to unburden her soul. The less said, the better.

The sun was touching the treetops when Pierce eased off the road into a parking area for one of the magnificent overlooks. In the distance, the valley sprawled like a sun-baked beauty, Charlottesville itself appearing peaceful and somnolent.

Pierce came around and opened her door. "Think you can walk?"

"I know I can." She got out and followed him to a lone picnic table situated to take advantage of the view.

Pierce patted the top. "Let's sit."

She joined him, for the first time feeling self-conscious about her appearance. She typically used her formal work clothing to induce clients to trust her and to make an unspoken statement about her educational achievements. Here, with Pierce, she looked more like someone's summer girlfriend. He, on the other hand, seemed confident and capable no matter what he wore.

As a man in his prime, he exuded a palpable masculinity that made a woman feel weak, especially at the end of a long, stressful day. Nikki had felt helpless too many times in her life. So if Pierce made her want to lean on him, he was definitely the wrong man to moon over.

When the silence between them grew too lengthy for comfort, she made herself interrupt the intimacy that seemed to bind them in a cocoon. "It's so beautiful." Humidity was high today, and the air, though by no means as bad as it had been earlier in the day, was still oppressive at this hour.

"You've been up here before, though. Right?"

"Of course. But it's been a while. I have a hard time with the concept of relaxation."

"Were you one of those kids who had to be perfect to please your parents?"

"No." He kept dancing around the issue, but so far he hadn't pressed for an explanation of her roots. "But I'm pretty hard on myself...or I have been in the past. Part of this six-week hiatus is self-examination. I may reinvent myself."

Pierce touched her briefly on the knee. "I kinda like you the way you are," he said laconically.

They were both staring straight ahead, aligned hip to hip and shoulder to shoulder, but not touching. The back of her neck was damp with sweat. Pierce radiated warmth. The smell of his clothing and aftershave was all male. Deliciously, tantalizingly male.

She clasped her hands in her lap. Sometimes these overlooks were crowded with tourists. But it was late in the day, and she and Pierce were all alone. That fact made her nervous. Not because of him, but because of her. A woman who could put aside a perfectly good job to play hooky for six weeks was obviously deranged. Capable of anything.

"Do you have a girlfriend?" The words popped out of her mouth without warning. When she gasped and pressed a hand over her lips, Pierce chuckled. He leaned back on his hands, the position straining the seams of his shirt. He was a big guy.

"Not at the moment," he said, his grin broad. Her question clearly pleased him. "Are you asking as my lawyer?"

"Of course," she huffed. "Why else would I want to know?"

"Maybe because you want me to kiss you."

"I do not." She glanced at the clear sky above to make sure no renegade lightning bolts had her in their sights.

"Do, too."

She jumped to her feet, forgetting about her injured toe. "Ouch." Pain spiked up her foot, but it was more of a dull ache now.

Pierce unfolded his big frame to stand beside her. He scooped her into his arms. "I want to kiss you, too," he said, the words husky and low. Goose bumps skittered up and down her arms as a ribbon of arousal tickled her spine. "Put your arms around my neck."

"I can walk," she insisted, hearing the steady thump of his heartbeat beneath her cheek. She curled one arm as he asked, but left the other free to feel the heat of his chest beneath her hand.

"But you don't need to when I'm here." His head lowered, his mouth hovering over hers. Leaning his butt against the picnic table for support, he found her lips with his, brushing them with a butterfly caress that made her squirm. The gentle kiss was torture when what she wanted was so shockingly *not* gentle.

He held her comfortably, but not so tightly that she couldn't have wriggled out of his hold if she had so chosen. "Kiss me again." Her bossy side took over.

His lips quirked. "I thought you didn't want me to kiss you."

"Don't gloat," she grumbled. "It's not attractive."

"But you are," he whispered. "Very attractive. Damned beautiful, in fact."

Since she didn't know what to say to that, she closed her eyes as his lips drifted from her brow to her eyelids to her nose, and finally, to her mouth.

"I think I must be dreaming," he groaned.

She couldn't help the little whimper that escaped her parted lips. The kiss was chaste, almost sweet…at least until her tongue darted out to toy with his. Pierce's body shook, and he muttered something under his breath before he grabbed her up, devouring her as if he hadn't kissed a woman in years. He was good, damned good. They went at each other, desperate, hungry. Incredulous, on her part. God knew what on his. Maybe this was how he initiated each new relationship.

"Stop." Somewhere, somehow, she summoned the presence of mind to call a halt before they both were arrested for indecent exposure. Pierce had begun unbuttoning her blouse, but he froze instantly at her ragged command. Breathing hard, he set her none too gently on the picnic table and stepped back to wipe his mouth with the back of his hand.

"I didn't start it."

His blunt, though implied, accusation made her laugh when she would have sworn that laughter was the furthest thing from her mind. "I never said you did. But I'd prefer not to appear before a judge as the accused. Five more minutes and we'd both have been—"

"In flagrante delicto?"

"Look at you and your legal terms."

"I learned that one in junior high…the summer my next-door neighbor began swiping his dad's adult-magazine collection."

She held up a hand. "Say no more. I'm not sure about the statute of limitations on that one."

Pierce crossed his arms over his chest, his feet planted shoulder width apart. "I think we've strayed from the subject at hand." He looked like a man ready for a good argument.

Lucky for her, arguing came as naturally as breathing. "There was no subject," she said calmly. "Just two people enjoying the view."

His gaze dropped deliberately to her chest. "Plenty to enjoy."

She felt her nipples bead into tight, achy nubs. The sensation was so acutely uncomfortable, she bit her lip. When Pierce got that look in his eyes, she could swear she was the sexiest woman on the planet. Since she had no script for such a scenario, she was winging it. And that made her nervous. Part of being a good lawyer involved preparation, preparation, preparation. Never getting caught unawares.

This *thing* with Pierce had caught her at a vulnerable time. Already emotionally off balance because of her career flux, she had not been ready to handle an acute case of sexual attraction.

And though she was pretty sure the feeling was mutual, Pierce wasn't exactly the picture of a man who was enjoying himself.

She pulled her knees up to her chest and linked her arms around them. "I can explain what just happened. It's really very simple."

Six

Pierce was frustrated. Hard and hurting. He knew Nikki had been right to call a halt to their very public fooling around. But that didn't mean he had to like it. "Do tell," he said. "I'm all ears."

Nikki, for once looking the tiniest bit mussed, managed a placating smile. "You're upset. And for a man, the easiest way to take your mind off your problems is to have sex."

"I haven't *had* sex," he pointed out with what he thought was monumental patience, considering the fact that he was a few breathless seconds away from pushing her down on that table and having his way with her.

Color warmed her cheeks. "I'd like to go home, please. We can talk more tomorrow. After a good night's sleep."

Pierce ground his jaw. "I'm not interested in talking."

She sighed. "I'm supposed to be helping you with a problem, not flirting."

"I'm pretty sure what we just did was a few degrees beyond flirting. And I don't need you telling me how to run my life."

"You *hired* me, remember?" A tiny frown wrinkle between her brows indicated that she was annoyed. Well, that was fine, because he was none too happy with her, either.

"Get in the car," he said. "I think the moment is lost, anyway."

The drive back to the city was completed in silence. He drove ten miles above the speed limit all the way, almost wishing he could get pulled over and have an altercation with a cop…anything to defuse the restless energy pin-balling in his veins.

Nikki sat, spine straight, in the passenger seat, staring out through the windshield. She had given up on trying to protect her hair—the wind whipped it in a hundred directions, giving her the look of a winsome biker chick ready to hit the road for parts unknown.

He had a feeling that such a summation was entirely fiction on his part. Nicola Parrish was an uptight, play-by-the-rules ballbuster. There was nothing spontaneous or fun about her.

Even as he told himself that, he knew he was lying. He was just in a bad mood because she'd been the sensible one. And to be honest, he was also uneasy when he acknowledged the fact that she had taken him to the edge at warp speed. Like a hormonal sixteen-year-old kid, he had been blind and deaf to everything but the demands of his body.

That admission sobered him. "I'm sorry," he said gruffly.

She shot him a look. "For what?"

"For being grumpy. You were right to stop me."

"I stopped *us*," she pointed out with a prissy tone that made him mad all over again. "You don't get to take all the credit for animalistic madness."

"God, you're aggravating." And so cute and sexy he could gobble her up with a spoon. He moved restlessly in the driver's seat. "I want to ask you a question, and I want the truth when you answer."

Her head swung around so fast she probably suffered whiplash. In the split second he glanced at her face, he saw alarm. "What question?"

"Those hospital records were basically a waste of time and money, right? We learned nothing."

Nikki looked away, giving him a vantage point of her classic profile with its perfect nose and slightly pointed chin. "Yes. That's true. But from a legal point of view, we had to start somewhere. I think the next move is up to you. This great-aunt you mentioned. Is she still alive?"

"Yes. She lives in a nursing home in Richmond. My mom visits Aunt Trudie once a month…or at least she did until Dad became so ill. I'm ashamed to say it, but my father and I haven't seen Trudie in several years. She's ninety-two. As far as I know, her mind is as sharp as it ever was."

He pulled up in front of Nikki's condo and shut off the engine. Half turning in his seat, he stared at her while she smoothed her hair into a semblance of order. "What now?" he asked, the fingers of his left hand drumming on the steering wheel.

Nikki grimaced. "I have a few things I need to take care of. Why don't you contact your aunt…set up a visit. Then call me with a plan."

"How soon can I call?"

Nikki got out and stood on the sidewalk, shutting the car door carefully. "Give me forty-eight hours. I'll wrap up my personal business and be ready to go. But I'll need my car."

"I'll drop it off in the morning. You could fix me breakfast," he added hopefully.

"I'm not much of a cook." She stared at him, heating his blood all over again. "You really are ridiculously handsome."

Pierce got out of the car and stood, keeping the vehicle

between them. "I could come upstairs and make sure everything is okay."

She wrinkled her nose. "Like what?"

Was she really so clueless?

"You know…burglars, monsters under the bed. That kind of thing."

"I'll be fine. I've been coming home at night by myself for a long, long time."

"I never asked you, did I?"

"Asked me what?"

"If you had a boyfriend…"

"You know I don't," she said simply. "A woman who has a boyfriend she cares about would never kiss a man like I just kissed you."

"Some would."

"Not me."

"Well, I'm glad, then."

"Why?"

"Because I'd have to run him off, and that would be cruel."

She smiled, and when she did, the whole world seemed brighter. It was a genuine, teasing smile that told him she didn't mind his braggadocio. "Go away now. Good night, Pierce."

He rounded the car and joined her on the sidewalk. Without waiting for permission, he slid his hands beneath her hair, cupped her head and angled it toward his for another kiss. His hands were shaking, and when he tasted her, his mind went blank. All he could do was feel. Her soft skin. Trembling lips. Silky hair that splayed over his fingers in a gentle caress.

Though he hadn't noticed when it happened, her arms were wrapped tightly around his waist. She was tall, but he was taller still. Her slight frame felt vulnerable, breakable in his embrace. A rush of tenderness overwhelmed him. "Ask me to come upstairs," he whispered, nipping the side of her neck with his teeth.

Nikki sagged against him, letting him support her weight. They were so close he knew she could feel his erection. "I can't do that," she said softly. "And once again, we're standing on a public thoroughfare. Do you ever kiss women in private?"

"Take me inside and I'll show you." He had meant the remark to be funny, but at the end his voice trailed off in a groan when one of Nikki's hands slid under the hem of his shirt and settled at his waist. The simple touch burned his bare flesh. "Enough." This time he was the one to put on the brakes. "Go inside. Now."

She pulled away, her eyes slightly unfocused and her pink lips puffy from his kisses. "I will." She backed up three steps. "Good night."

"I'll bring you medicine for your toe in the morning when I come."

"I might sleep in. Just leave it in the car."

"You're afraid of me."

"Yes."

Her candor stopped him cold. "You don't have to be. I'm as trustworthy as a Boy Scout. I *was* one, in fact."

"Not that kind of scared. I'm afraid I'll let you distract me from working on my life plan."

"I'm hurt." Not altogether a lie.

"You're pushy."

"Takes one to know one."

"I'm fairly certain we may kill each other if we keep this up."

"I'll say it again—you don't have to be afraid of me." He made himself turn around and walk over to her car. When he slid into the driver's seat and glanced back, she was gone.

* * *

Nikki changed into her comfiest pajamas, found a favorite old chick flick on cable and snuggled into the corner of her sofa. At times like this she wished she had a pet, but she worked such odd hours, it seemed unkind to leave an animal shut up inside all day.

Instead of turning up the sound, she put on the closed captions so she could follow the story in silence. Her head was spinning with a million thoughts and conundrums. What had happened to Pierce when he was an infant? Was his mother lying? Would Pierce be terribly upset when and if they found out the truth? And would that end any contact Nikki had with him?

Did he really want to sleep with her, or was it a matter of serendipity? Did he subconsciously believe that if they became lovers she wouldn't press so hard for answers?

On the screen, Meg Ryan, wearing a small gray cardigan and a lemon-yellow dress, smiled her trademark smile, and the hero melted. Nikki knew the feeling. She considered herself a tough, sometimes cynical realist. But something about Pierce Avery reduced her to a teenage angst she hadn't experienced for a long, long time. This feeling of being completely off balance was difficult to deal with. Especially since he really did want to use her professional services.

And then there was the tiny matter of her job. She couldn't get sidetracked at such a pivotal moment. It would be really easy to let herself fall into a purely physical relationship with Pierce. Most women would be hard-pressed to say no to him. But if Nikki used sex to avoid dealing with the big questions she had posed for herself, she'd be doing both Pierce and herself a disservice.

When the movie ended two hours later, she glanced

sleepily at her watch. Instead of heading for the bedroom, she reached for a couple of afghans and a throw pillow, got comfortable and closed her eyes. No reason to set an alarm. Because although she had a lengthy to-do list for tomorrow, the day was completely unscripted. No one but another control freak could understand how much that lack of structure dismayed her.

The last thing she recalled before falling asleep was the way Pierce's eyes crinkled at the edges when he smiled....

Pierce waited thirty-six hours before calling his new lawyer. She had told him forty-eight, but he was anxious not to lose another day. In the small amount of time since he had been with Nikki, he'd had a disturbing conversation with his mother. Though his father had stabilized, the stress of the long hospital stay combined with the secret she was keeping from her spouse had frazzled her. Because of that, Pierce decided he had to be on his best behavior from now on. No hanky-panky with Nicola Parrish.

His first priority had to be finding out the truth about his parentage.

But when Nikki answered the phone on the third ring, his heartbeat stuttered and sped up. She sounded as if she had just climbed out of bed, and his imagination jumped into the game, painting pictures of a long-legged blonde with an attitude...wearing only baby-doll pajamas and a smile.

It was laughable, really. He was pretty sure that women only wore those in 1960s movies. But the image stayed with him nevertheless.

He cleared his throat. "I've got everything all set up. Can you be ready to leave at eight in the morning?"

There was a brief pause and then the sound of rustling paper. "I can."

"I've booked two hotel rooms in case we need to stay over. Why don't you bring some casual clothes and a swimsuit? Aunt Trudie naps a lot, from what I recall, so we may have to interview her in spurts. It could take longer than we think it will."

"Have you talked to your aunt directly?"

"Mom called her and said I was coming for a visit. Obviously, we don't want to upset her. She may not even remember all the details. It was a long time ago and she's really old."

"Pierce?"

"Yeah?"

"What are you going to do if this is a dead end?"

His stomach pitched and rolled. He hadn't let himself think about that. "I'll cross that bridge when I come to it. To be honest, I don't care if I ever know. I'm doing this for my mom."

"You may think that, but it's not true. Whether you like it or not, the questions will never go away. I'll be ready in the morning. Try not to worry."

After a sleepless night, Pierce crawled out of bed and used a cold shower to wake himself up. He was jittery and a little bit scared. The chances of his great-aunt really having any valuable info was slim, but other than Pierce's own mom and dad, she was the only person present when he was born who might shed some light on this untenable situation.

He had thrown most of his gear in a bag the night before, so all he had to do was put together his shave kit and grab breakfast. One glance inside his refrigerator told him he was out of luck. Feeling hopeful and hungry, he sent a text to Nikki.

Brkfst on the road??

Her reply was prompt and funny.

The mrning aftr w/o the nite b4...interesting...

Suddenly his resolution to be all business weakened. He was going to spend the day with an intelligent, beautiful woman who entertained him endlessly. Not a bad way to start.

When he pulled up in front of Nikki's and parked, she walked out the front door of her building. Apparently she'd been watching for him. And maybe thinking she shouldn't let him inside. Probably a good plan.

He'd brought a more conventional car today. Popping the trunk, he hopped out and took her bags. "Need any of this up front?"

She shook her head. "Nope. But that breakfast better not be far or I'm going to get really cranky."

"Not to worry." He chuckled as he closed her door and strode around to the other side to get in. "It's a hole-in-the-wall diner just outside of town. A lot of the local farmers patronize it, so you know it has to be good."

Over rashers of crisp bacon, perfectly scrambled eggs and an endless pot of coffee, he studied his accomplice. She was wearing black slacks with a matching jacket and a turquoise blouse that somehow looked even better framed in a red vinyl booth. She'd barely spoken to him for five minutes as she dug into her food. He reached across the table and tapped her arm. "I'll feed you again in a few hours."

She lifted one eyebrow. "Are you insinuating that I'm eating too much?"

He held up his hands. "Not at all. I like a woman who enjoys her food."

"I burn it off…lots of nervous energy."

Suddenly it was as if every noise in the crowded diner receded, leaving the two of them in a bubble of silence.

Nikki's fair skin turned red from her throat to her hairline. She had clearly not intended her toss-away comment to sound sexual. But he had heard it that way, and she knew he had.

Pierce ran a hand through his hair. "I think we'd better talk about it."

She stirred her grits, staring at her plate as if the answer to all of life's thorny questions could be discerned in a swirl of redeye gravy. "Talk about what?"

He shook his head, leaning back in his seat with a grin. "You know what. This ill-timed attraction."

"I don't know what you mean. That sounds like a bad TV-movie title."

"I'm serious, Nikki. I told myself yesterday that all I was going to concentrate on was solving this damned riddle I'm facing. But when I'm with you, I can't seem to work up any interest in my parentage. All I can think about is how soon we're going to end up in bed together."

She lifted her head, her eyes darker than usual, the pupils dilated. "Are we?" she asked with a lopsided smile.

"I hope so." He laid it all out on the table. "I never imagined this when I showed up in your office, but it's almost impossible to ignore. I promised I'd help you unwind. That didn't include sex when I said it, but it does now."

She leaned her head on one hand, elbow on the table. "You're very direct."

"I know what I want."

"We're nothing alike, Pierce. And to be honest, it's not

my style to sleep with a man when I know there's no future in it."

"Why do you say that?"

"Oh, come on. Surely you're not that blind. You work outdoors for a living. Kayaking, rappelling, camping. I can't swim, I'm afraid of heights and I hate bugs. We are about as far apart as two people can be."

"So you're telling me that a guy has to pass a marriage test before you'll have sex with him?"

"Of course not. First of all, I haven't had sex with that many men. I'm fairly fastidious in my choices of who to date, because my time is precious, and I choose not to spend it with people who don't appeal to me."

"Do I fall into that category?"

"Are you fishing for compliments?"

"Maybe I am." And it stunned him that he cared so much what she thought of him.

"I think you're sexy and fun and a genuinely nice guy, though I know men don't like to hear that last one. You're in a bad place in your life, but you're not doing the whole *why me* thing. You seem to care what your mother wants and needs, which I find charming. And even though you dislike lawyers in general, you've given me a chance to prove that not all of us are slime. On a scale of one to ten, I give you a solid eight."

His jaw dropped. "Only an eight after that rousing list of attributes?"

She smirked. "You lose ground when it comes to arrogance and patience."

She had him there. "Fair enough. But what you're saying is that we shouldn't have sex because we want different things out of life."

"I suppose you could put it that way."

He shrugged and lifted a hand for their check. When the

waitress scurried over with a smile, he glanced at the bill, pulled out two twenties and told her to keep the change.

While he settled the tab, Nikki had finished eating and was studying their fellow patrons. It was definitely a blue-collar crowd, which meant that she and Pierce, dressed as they were, stood out. He stood up and held out a hand. "We'd better get going."

She put her hand in his without hesitation, making his mouth dry and his whole body tense. If such simple contact affected him so deeply, he was up a creek without a paddle. The old adage hit home to someone who actually knew what that felt like. Getting knocked around in fast-moving water, unable to steer. It was scary as hell.

In the car, Nikki fussed with her seat belt and sat back with a sigh. "Aren't you going to argue with me about this thing between us? Tell me I should go with the flow?"

He rested his hands on the wheel, the car still in Park. Not looking at her at all, he was still intensely aware of her scent, her mood, the sound of her voice. "Should I?"

She yanked on her blond tresses. "This is me pulling my hair out. I don't know what you want me to say."

"Don't say anything," he said, his mood souring as he realized how close he was to a revelation he didn't want or need. "If it's going to happen, it will. In the meantime, let's get this other mess over with. My life is a freaking soap opera, and I'd just as soon end this episode one way or another."

Seven

Nikki turned on the satellite radio, tuning it to a channel that played a mix of classic rock and newer music. Pierce had lapsed into silence, and she needed something for a distraction. The trip from Charlottesville was barely an hour and a half. Which was a good thing, because she could feel his tension growing mile by mile.

It was going to be an incredible letdown for him if his aunt was clueless. But Nikki had an uneasy suspicion that this whole mystery led back to that night in the hospital when Pierce was born. An old woman just might be the only key to unlocking the past.

Unfortunately, the lawyer in her couldn't resist asking questions. Besides, it might do Pierce good to talk. Surely that was better than whatever battles he was fighting in his head.

"Tell me about your great-aunt," she said. "Why are she and your mother close?"

It was several long seconds before he answered, as if his thoughts had been far away. He signaled for a lane change, passed a slow-moving pickup truck and pulled back to the right. "My maternal grandmother died of pneumonia when my mom was four years old. My grandfather came from a generation of men who didn't think child-rearing was their responsibility. So enter Aunt Gertrude. She was a decade older than my grandmother, the much-older sister, and she had already married and divorced when my mom was born. It was a big scandal, because she had also defied tradition and gone to medical school. Many in the family thought that was to blame for the failure of her marriage, or so I've been told."

"Did she have any children?"

"One daughter. Because Aunt Gertrude didn't think Mom should have to lose both parents, she moved her own child to Charlottesville, bought a house, got a job in obstetrics at one of the local hospitals and then took my mom in."

"Wow. That's dedication."

"It was. And as far as I can tell, my mother has in every way regarded Gertrude as her actual mother."

"Wouldn't it be kind of weird to have your mother figure deliver your baby?"

"Not in the frontier days probably, but in modern times, yes. Gertrude wasn't my mom's doctor, though. Apparently, when Mom went into labor, there had been a flu outbreak. Dozens of nurses and doctors had fallen ill, so everyone not on duty at the hospital that night was called in for relief. I've heard the story a dozen times. Aunt Gertrude, in her early sixties when I was born, single-handedly ran the emergency room and the OB ward for thirty-six hours straight."

"I can't wait to meet her," Nikki said, trying to imagine such a thing. "She must be an incredible woman."

"She definitely is. I imagine the two of you will have a lot in common."

It wasn't long until the outskirts of Richmond came into view. Pierce's agitation was almost palpable, his hands white-knuckled on the steering wheel. The nursing home where his aunt lived was located in a pleasant community with mature trees, flower gardens and lots of middle-class houses. He parked in the visitor lot and sat stone-faced for long seconds.

Nikki touched his shoulder. "Let's go in. Sitting here won't make you feel any better."

With a muttered curse, he got out of the car and followed her to the front door. "She's bound to know something is up," he said. "Over the years I've spent time with her on holidays at her daughter's house, but never here. It's been a long time since I've seen her."

"Doesn't matter. I know she'll be happy to have a visit from her great-nephew."

Inside, the atmosphere was calm and reasonably cheerful. An institution was still an institution, and the usual smells of cafeteria food and cleaning supplies mingled with a less pervasive liniment aroma. When Pierce identified himself at the front desk and asked for directions, the staff was friendly and professional.

Fortunately, Gertrude's room was not far away. Down one hall and around the corner. Nikki stood back as Pierce knocked quietly.

"Come in." The quavering voice was weak.

Nikki made Pierce go first, despite his gentlemanly inclination to hold the door for her. She followed him in and lingered by the exit, her stomach in a knot as she watched the encounter.

Gertrude was sitting in a wheelchair near the window, fully dressed in a pale-blue polyester pantsuit that hung on her bony frame. Snow-white hair framed a face that was more suited to a man than a woman, because of its blunt features. A large nose and snapping black eyes added up to a visage that once upon a time must have commanded respect and attention.

Even seated, it was clear Gertrude was a tall woman. Her shoulders were bent and her gnarled hands lay loosely clasped in her lap, but her attitude was completely alert. She didn't smile when she saw Pierce. If anything, she paled somewhat.

"Hello, Aunt Gertrude." Pierce bent awkwardly and gave her a hug. He waved a hand in Nikki's direction. "This is my friend Nicola Parrish. I hope you don't mind that I brought her along."

"Of course not. Hello, young woman. Are you two an item?"

Nikki sputtered, waiting for Pierce to save her. When he did not, she shot him a dirty look. "No, ma'am. We're just friends."

"With benefits, you mean? I stay up with modern jargon. Can't keep the brain healthy if all you do is watch *Jeopardy* and the *Wheel*. I read three newspapers every day, and when I'm able, I go down to the computer lab and look up something on Google that I need to learn about."

Nikki decided the friends-with-benefits question was rhetorical, so she kept silent and let Pierce take over.

He pulled up a stool and sat beside his aunt. "How are you feeling, Aunt Trudie?"

She patted his hand, her weathered features alight with mischief. "Good days and bad. When you get to be ninety-two, just pooping is a victory."

Pierce's face was priceless. Nikki worked so hard to hold back a laugh that her eyes watered.

He tried to recover, but it was clear he was rattled. "Do you have friends here?"

"A couple. They keep dying on me. It's not a picnic when you outlive all your generation. Don't know why the good

Lord is still keeping me here, but as long as he is, I may as well do what I can. Had to teach a seminar last week to these old coots about STDs and HIV. You'd be shocked to know what goes on here when the lights are out."

Pierce, with a small grin on his face, got to his feet and looked out the window where a rose garden was hanging on to a few last blooms. "I'm glad you're keeping busy," he said.

For a long moment, Nikki thought he was going to chicken out. But she should have known better. Pierce might not want to be here, but he was a strong man, a courageous one. And he had made a promise to his mother to follow this through.

Though he might not want to admit it, somewhere deep in his gut, he was doing this for himself as well.

He rested a hand on the glass, sighed deeply and turned around, leaning back against the windowsill. "I need to talk to you, Aunt Trudie. About something important."

Her smile faded, and every ounce of animation in her demeanor evaporated. "About what?" Leathery fingers clenched the armrests of her chair.

"The night I was born."

Without warning, her eyes rolled back in her head and she slumped to one side in a dead faint.

Pierce reached for her, steadying her so she didn't tumble out of the chair. Nikki searched frantically for a call button, found it and paged a nurse. "Room seven thirteen. Come quickly. The patient has passed out."

The next half hour was chaotic. Medics were on the scene in minutes. After stabilizing Gertrude, they lifted her as carefully as if she was their own kin, strapped her to a gurney, wheeled her down the hall and loaded her into the waiting ambulance.

Pierce and Nikki ran for the car and followed behind.

At the hospital, the hours passed with agonizing slowness. Once it was determined that Gertrude would be admitted to intensive care, Pierce was tied up on the phone with the nursing home for half an hour dealing with formalities. He also had to call his mother, who was frantic because she couldn't leave his father. Gertrude's daughter had passed away three years earlier from complications after a hysterectomy, so Pierce's mom was her next of kin.

By the time he slumped into a chair in the waiting room, Nikki was worried about him. Stress had carved deep grooves between his eyebrows and at the corners of his mouth. She sat down beside him and handed him a cup of coffee. "Drink this. And tell me what you want to eat." Breakfast had been hours ago, and they had skipped lunch entirely.

"I'm not hungry."

She let that slide for the moment. Pierce hadn't fully met her stubborn side yet. "What's your mother going to do?"

"Nothing now. I'm supposed to keep her updated."

Nikki glanced at her watch. "ICU has visitation in about five minutes and then not again until eight tonight. Do you want to sign in and see her?"

He leaned back his head and closed his eyes, his cup resting on his chest. "What if seeing me upsets her? They said she had some kind of mini stroke."

"It's not your fault. She's ninety-two."

He shot to his feet, threw the cup in the trash with enough force to rock the small metal can and beat a fist on the wall. "She knows," he said, his voice hoarse. "She knows what happened. I could see it on her face. And if she dies, I'll never have the truth." He clenched both fists, the cords in his neck standing out, his eyes filled with anguish. "I should be worried about my aunt, and I am, but all I can think about is that if we lose her now, I'm screwed."

Nikki already liked Pierce Avery. A lot. But seeing him

like this tapped into something she knew a lot about. The fear. The anger. The feeling of betrayal and loss. A great wave of empathy and compassion flooded her with a need to comfort him any way she could.

"Let's go check in to the hotel," she said quietly. "The hospital has your number. It doesn't make sense to stay here right now."

As they walked out to the car, she stopped him. "I think I should drive. You're in no shape to be behind the wheel."

He started to argue. She could see it in his eyes. But after long, taut seconds, he handed over the keys and got in opposite her. She had to pull the seat up a long way, but when she was comfortable, she looked at him. "Do you know where the hotel is, or do you want me to use the GPS?"

"I'll direct you. It's not far."

In less than fifteen minutes, they pulled into the semi-circular driveway of an upscale downtown hotel. "I would have been fine with a motel near the interstate," she said, realizing that he would insist on paying for both rooms.

"This will be more pleasant."

Nikki didn't have to lift a finger as a bellman loaded their luggage from the trunk onto a cart. Pierce tipped the man generously and took Nikki's elbow. "Let's go check in."

It was the middle of the week and several conventions were in town, but the desk clerk handed them two keys with a smile. "We tucked you both away from the crowd. If anyone disturbs you, please let us know."

Pierce proffered his credit card, and the deed was done. Riding up the elevator, he was silent. Aloof. Totally turned inward. Nikki ached for him. His whole world had been turned on its ear in a matter of days. It was amazing that he was still capable of functioning. She knew what stress could do to a person.

When they got off on their floor, a different bellman was

waiting for them. He took Nikki's things into one room, and
Pierce's into the adjoining one. Another tip and then suddenly Nikki found herself standing in the hall, awkwardly
wondering what her role should be in all this drama. Perhaps the most she could do for Pierce was establish nor-
malcy for a little bit.

She had to say his name twice to get his attention. When
he looked at her, she smiled gently. "Why don't you order
room service for both of us? I'm not picky. I'll grab a quick
shower and change into jeans. Then I'll come over in about
thirty minutes, eat with you and tell you the story of my
life."

That last bit actually seemed to snap him out of his fog.
"You will?"

She nodded. "I think it's time."

After her shower, she stood beside the bed, suitcase open
wide, and surveyed her choices. She had packed one set
of nice lingerie, knowing that as persuasive as Pierce was
and with the powerful attraction that just wouldn't seem to
go away, there was a better-than-average chance she might
choose to be intimate with him.

Even now, she wasn't sure. But just in case, she slipped
into the pale-blue camisole and matching bikini panties. She
hadn't needed to wash her hair, so she combed it, brushed
her teeth and spritzed a tiny bit of her favorite scent at her
throat and wrists. The jeans she had packed were old, soft
and faded. She topped them with a button-up shirt of crisp
white cotton and rolled up the sleeves.

Her toe was still a little sore. Since the hotel was plenty
warm, she left her feet bare. Standing in front of the connecting door that linked the two rooms, she gnawed her
bottom lip. Lots of hotels had access like this, but normally

the doors stayed locked on both sides unless rooms were booked by family groups.

Had Pierce requested this setup, or was it a happy accident?

She unlocked her side as quietly as possible. After several minutes of dithering, she decided she didn't have the courage to knock. Such an action indicated a level of intimacy that didn't feel entirely comfortable to her. Her only choice was to grab her key card, go out into the hall and rap her knuckles on the outer door.

Pierce answered immediately. "You're right on time. The food just got here." He was barefoot as well and had changed out of his dress slacks and shirt into comfy clothes similar to her own.

"Something smells good." The room had a small sitting area with a foldout sofa and a coffee table. Pierce had arranged their meal there.

He waited for her to sit and then took the opposite end. "I thought hamburgers were a safe choice. The menu said they were Angus, so I hope they're good."

An odd awkwardness had bloomed between them in the hours since breakfast. She suspected it was because he didn't like anyone seeing him vulnerable, so he had pulled back emotionally.

"I'm sure they're fine." And they were. Delicious, in fact. What wasn't fine was the weight of all they weren't saying. She took a swallow of water and wiped her lips. "Has the hospital called?"

He kept eating, his attention on his food. "I called them. She's stable."

"That's good."

"Yeah."

She scooted closer and put her arm around his back.

"Talk to me, Pierce. If you keep it bottled up inside you, you'll explode."

He paused, burger in hand, and glared at her. "So now you're a lawyer *and* a shrink?"

The question had a definite bite. But she wouldn't let him bait her. "I'm just a listening ear. Be mad at me if it helps, but for the moment, I'm the only backup you've got."

Eight

Pierce abandoned his food, feeling a lick of shame. Deliberately standing up so she couldn't touch him, he paced. He owed her an apology. Nikki had stood by him all during this long, lousy day. She'd been a rock, in fact. Calm and cool as a summer lake with no wind.

As a sportsman, he preferred white-water rapids and the challenge of a dangerous passage. But at the moment, a becalmed sea sounded mighty appealing. He shoved his hands in his pockets and sat on the edge of the king-sized bed. "I'm sorry I snapped at you," he said gruffly. "I have no excuse other than the fact that I don't like feeling out of control, and this situation is kicking my ass."

"I appreciate the apology, but I do understand. What are you going to do?"

He shrugged, wishing he knew. "If she gets to go home, I'll just wait and try again. Who knows how long they'll keep her."

"I hate to add to your plate, but what if she refuses to tell you anything, or says she doesn't know?"

Nikki's unspoken sympathy smoothed some of the raw

edges of his mood. "I don't think she can look me in the eye and lie to me. You saw her face. That woman knows why I'm not an Avery. I don't wish her ill, but if she is at all stable and cognizant, I *am* going to ask again."

"I don't blame you. I would do the same."

In her eyes he saw something more than sympathy—he saw genuine empathy. As if she had walked this road. But that was impossible. No two families could have faced the same unbelievable revelation. A son who wasn't a son. Even Pierce's mother was baffled.

He leaned back on his elbows. "You promised me a story," he said, trying to shake off his dismal mood. Nikki looked as beautiful as ever. He couldn't imagine what he would have done without her to help him wade through this mess.

She crossed her legs, her bare toes with the pale-pink polish making him remember suddenly that there was more at stake than his parentage. He'd made his intentions pretty clear when it came to his needs and desires. Would Nikki reciprocate, or was he doomed to want her endlessly?

His dinner guest eyed him sternly. "Are you okay, Pierce?"

"Just peachy." She didn't like his sarcasm, he could tell.

"There's no sin in talking about it."

"No offense, Nikki, but I can handle it. Hashing it out would make things worse. Tell me your tale. I'm ready to listen."

She pulled her knees to her chest in a move he had come to recognize. "I grew up in a church-run children's home." For a brief moment, the confident woman disappeared and he caught a glimpse of bone-deep grief. But it was gone so quickly he told himself he was imagining angst where there was none.

He sat up, hands on his knees. "I didn't know. I'm sorry. How did your parents die?"

"I have no idea. Actually, I'm pretty sure one or both of them was alive until I was about thirteen. Because every time I asked why I couldn't be adopted, I was told that it wasn't possible. When I finally became *eligible,* it was too late. No one wants to adopt a sullen, adolescent girl."

He felt as if someone had ripped up a script and told him to improvise. He gazed at her, stunned. "But you went to Harvard." It was all he could think of to say, but she didn't call him out on his dumb statement.

"Turns out I was freakishly smart. There was a social worker who took an interest in me and helped with scholarships and stuff."

"What about high school?"

"It was a nightmare," she said. "I was the girl with the ten-year-old hand-me-down clothes…and everyone knew who the kids were from the children's home. It was a small town with very few secrets. I was never invited to a party, never attended a sleepover. No dances. No prom dresses. But I survived."

She hadn't dressed it up, but the recitation touched him deeply. How could a woman as strong and smart and capable as Nicola Parrish have come from such modest beginnings?

He stood and joined her on the small sofa, wanting to be near her. "Do you know anything at all about your parents?"

"Not one damn thing." She stopped. "Sorry. I usually can talk about this without getting angry. I guess what happened today brought a lot of it back." Her eyes shone with tears, but not one fell. "I think the reason I became a lawyer was to have the credentials to track down my roots. But in the state of my birth, and in many other states, sealed records are sealed forever. Even if the person who requested that arrangement is deceased. Though I was never adopted, whoever placed me in the children's home in the beginning insisted I not know the identity of my parents. I had a friend with medical issues who desperately needed info about her biological father. She actually had a name and knew the man was dead, but the state would not give her access to his medical records."

He stared at her, saw the beauty, the confidence, the quiet efficiency. This woman was the whole package. Yet somewhere, somehow, someone had given up the right to call her their own. "I don't know what to say," he said. "Are you still investigating?"

"No. Not anymore. I came close to a breakdown in my early twenties. I became so fixated on finding the truth that I made myself ill. It took a year of counseling to help me see that the past was going to have to stay buried. Who my parents were, why they didn't want me, how they died…all of it an unsolved mystery."

"I can't even imagine what you went through."

"Let's just say that when you told me you didn't want to know who your real father was, it made me angry and sad. If all of this plays out like I think it will, you're going to find that you have not one but two families who love you. Two, Pierce. The people who raised you won't care if some accident or deliberate malice brought you to them. You *are* their son in every way that counts. And if we discover the identity of your biological parents, they will likely be thrilled to have a man like you as a son as well. It's a win-win as far as I can see. You're far luckier than you know."

From where she was sitting it must certainly seem so. And he knew what she was saying made sense, particularly given her past. But try as he might, the overwhelming emotions he felt were grief and loss over the destruction of his personal life story. On top of that was a helpless guilt that his parents had somehow lost the child who was supposed to be theirs. Pierce was an impostor.

He put aside his own turmoil. Gathering Nikki in his arms, he tucked her head to his chest, stroking her hair. "Come here, my lovely lady lawyer. Let me hold you."

She didn't protest, didn't say anything, in fact. All she did was nestle against him, her arms sliding around his waist.

He held her tightly, his brain whirling with images of both of them as children. Pierce remembered the pride with which his parents had displayed his trophies for soccer and field-day races. The many times they'd sat in an elementary-school auditorium and witnessed plays and speeches and awards nights.

Truth be told, his *parents* should have received the accolades. He hadn't been an easy child, but they had kept him on the straight and narrow, loving him too much to settle for excuses about why he wasn't getting his schoolwork done. Hour by hour, day by day, week by week they had worked with him until he had the confidence to believe he wasn't dumb, but in fact was actually pretty smart.

Who had done that for Nikki? No one in her formative years. Thank God for the social worker who helped her transition to college. What funds had Nikki lived off of? Who paid the bills? From what he knew of her, it had been Nikki and no one else. He wouldn't be surprised to hear that she'd held down two or three jobs while studying and making straight A's at an Ivy League school.

He played with her hair, loving the texture, the scent. Gradually, his body began to acknowledge that a lovely, sexy woman was curled up on his lap. His breathing grew hoarse. His arms trembled. His sex flexed and thickened. This wasn't the time for carnal thoughts. All he wanted to do was comfort her as she had comforted him.

But his body had other ideas. Gently, he began to ease

her out of his embrace. She clung tightly, even as he tried to escape.

"Don't go," she whispered. "I like it here. You feel good."

He sucked in a breath, hoping he was strong enough to cuddle her without taking things further. She deserved tenderness. More than anyone he knew.

There came a distinct moment when she realized why he was trying to let her go. She sat up suddenly, her cheeks flushed and her eyes heavy lidded. "Pierce?"

"Sorry," he said, his tone wry. "I was trying to be sensitive."

Nikki grinned at him, a gamine smile that tugged at his heartstrings. "Screw sensitive. I want you to take me to bed."

He froze. Was this some kind of test? "Um, well…" His vocabulary dried up along with the inside of his mouth. The air in the room grew thin.

Nikki took one of his hands and placed it on her breast. "I like you more than any man I've met in a long time. You make me feel things. Good things. Fun things. And no, I haven't changed my opinion of how ill-suited we are to be a couple, but it's been a long day, and I'd like to be with you tonight."

Simple. Direct. Painfully honest. He had to swallow twice before he could speak. "I'd like that, too."

She smiled at him, just a smile. And though she didn't realize it, she ripped his heart right out of his chest.

He ran his finger from her collarbone to the place where a row of buttons started down her chest. "Your lawyer suits make me hot," he muttered, "but I like this look, too.…" He unfastened her blouse slowly, unable to hear anything but his own heart beating. Nikki's gaze was downcast, her eyes shielded by thick lashes tipped in gold.

When he folded back the sides of the fabric, he saw that she was wearing a silky camisole. Her breasts were small but perfect, the nipples lifting against the paper-thin fabric. "You're so lovely, you make me ache," he said, reverence in his voice.

Finally, she looked at him, her cheeks pink. "I know I should work out. I suppose you're used to being with athletic women."

He chuckled as he removed the blouse completely. "I've never seen a more perfect body." Her skin was pale and smooth, and she was curved in all the right places. She wasn't wearing a bra beneath the camisole, so he entertained himself for long minutes just stroking the swells that were so beautifully feminine.

Nikki's head fell back against his arm, her eyes closed, her lips parted as she breathed heavily. "Feel free to take that off," she said, the words barely audible.

He knew better. Desire was a train barreling down the track. If he had any chance of slowing things down, he needed to keep her dressed as long as possible. "Patience, my Nikki. We'll get there." But in truth, he needed more room for what he had in mind, and a giant bed lay not ten feet away.

His own impatience growing, he scooted out from under his delightful burden and stood, lifting her in his arms. In three quick strides, he deposited her on the mattress, abandoning her only long enough to remove his belt for comfort. His shirt and pants he left in place to ensure he didn't rush this first time, when he wanted so badly to show her a slow, tender loving.

Nikki startled him by shimmying out of her jeans. The panties that matched her little top were barely more than two triangles covering her most intimate secrets. She threw back the covers and stretched out on the bed, arms over her head, palms to the ceiling. One leg was bent at the knee, her foot propped against her butt. "I'm counting on you for stamina," she said with a naughty grin. "All that aerobic exercise you do must count for something."

He laughed hoarsely, hunger riding him hard. Nikki challenged him and made him laugh. A combination he hadn't expected in the bedroom, but one that was damned arousing. "I knew there was a reason to stay in shape." He sprawled on his side next to her, putting one hand, fingers splayed, on her flat belly.

Nikki's eyelids fluttered shut. "Pierce…"

The way she groaned his name made the hair stand up on the back of his neck. What a surprise to find out that beneath the ladylike facade of the driven lawyer was a sensual woman with a kick-ass body and a knack for driving him crazy in the bedroom.

Slowly, tormenting them both, he slid his hand down the slick fabric of the camisole until his fingertips reached the edge of her almost-not-there undies. "Do you want me to touch you?" he asked.

Her hips lifted in a silent plea. "Yes. You know I do."

The hint of imperious demand made him grin, but she couldn't see it, because her eyes were squeezed shut, a tiny frown of concentration marring her perfect brow.

Instead of trespassing beneath the elastic band, he stroked two fingers downward, over the cloth, and pressed gently where the fabric was warm and damp. Nikki shuddered, panting but silent. He played with her…light, teasing strokes and then firm pressure, but backed off before she could reach what she wanted.

She grabbed his wrist. "I need more." The demand held little heat, because her words were slurred with pleasure.

"All in good time, my sweet. All in good time."

But he, too, fell victim to impatience. Sitting up only long enough to drag her camisole up and over her head, he lay down with her again, this time propped on his elbow so he could explore what he had uncovered. Her nipples were raspberry pink, just begging for a taste. When he took her in his mouth, they both moaned.

Rolling his tongue around one little nub, he felt the flesh pucker even more tightly. When he lightly scraped his teeth over the sensitive skin, Nikki caught her breath. Her eyes opened, and she smiled at him drowsily. "I might have been wrong about that eight ranking," she whispered. "You're climbing the charts every second."

As he moved from one breast to the other, he nodded. "I do have a competitive streak." He stayed tanned year-round from his many hours outdoors, and the contrast between his masculine hand and her soft, womanly skin was both erotic and fascinating. He traced her collarbone, the underside of her chin and back south to the shallow indentation of her navel.

Every touch made her sigh. But if his tactile exploration gave her pleasure, it gave him twofold in return. He was so hard he ached and shuddered with the need to move between her legs. It was too soon, though. He wasn't finished with her.

Making his way south once again, he removed her underwear entirely. Seeing her smooth shaven was both a shock and an intense turn-on. He fingered her mound, loving the plump curve of it, and lower—the moist, pink folds of her sex. He slid a finger downward, not entering her, only skating across her clitoris and separating the petals below.

He inhaled the scent of her arousal, felt it in the rigidity of her limbs, heard it in her choppy breathing. Seeing the swollen, glistening evidence told him only one sensory gift was left to unwrap. Taste.

Nikki made no protest when he moved lower in the bed. Now he could no longer toy with her breasts, but the consolation prize was as good or better. He rested his head on her upper thigh, enjoying the view. It was spectacular, though he wanted her too badly to linger long. Using both hands to spread her legs wide, he kissed her intimately, teasing her with his tongue.

Nikki cried out, not in climax but in shock. He knew there was more room for pleasure. "Slow, honey, slow." He thought if he kept his attentions light and irregular, she would linger on a knife edge of wanting. But when he stroked her long and slow with his tongue, she came instantly, her hands fisting in his hair and her body trembling violently as her skin flushed pink from head to toe.

Feeling something akin to a seismic shift, he scrambled up in the bed and moved on top of her, kissing her wildly. "Nikki, Nikki, Nikki…" He felt his control slipping away.

She opened her eyes, the irises cloudy and dark. Touching his lips with two fingers, she demanded his attention. "I think it's about time for you to take off your clothes, Mr. Avery."

Nine

Nikki was in trouble. Earlier in the diner, when she'd told Pierce she hadn't had sex with "that many men," she might have given him the wrong impression. There had actually been only three, and two of those hardly counted. During a particularly bad period in high school, she'd let herself be pressured into sex, twice, with two different boys, each time searching desperately for someone to love her. Both experiences had been pretty awful, and thankfully she'd been smart enough to demand they wear protection, so there had been no consequences other than a lingering feeling of depression and shame.

It wasn't until her last year of law school that she had tried again, and on that occasion she'd had reason to hope her new beau might be the real deal. With a seven-month relationship under her belt, she had honestly believed she was finally going to get her happily-ever-after. Unfortunately, when it came time to take the bar exam, she'd passed with flying colors and her lover had not even made the minimum required score. Things had gotten ugly after that, and once again she'd found herself alone. Since then she had dated on and off, but intimacy was not on the table. Until today.

Now she had found the kind of man every woman dreamed about, but she and Pierce were wrong for each other in almost every way.

She watched him stand up. His face was tightly drawn, and as he ripped off his shirt, she could see the muscles in his chest and arms cord and bunch. His skin was golden bronze. When he unzipped and shucked his pants and boxers, a strip of white at his hips was the only indication he didn't go commando in the great outdoors.

His penis reared proud and strong against his flat belly. Its length and girth made her shiver, either in anticipation or anxiety, or perhaps a dollop of both. Even in the aftermath of a truly spectacular orgasm, she wanted him so badly she was trembling.

When he was completely nude, he stared at her. "I'm afraid this one's gonna be pretty fast. We'll go for aerobic stamina the second time around...okay?"

"Already planning an encore?" She'd die before admitting that his arrogance gave her heart a little pitty-pat rhythm.

His eyes narrowed as his gaze scanned her from head to toe. "You have no idea, Nikki, no idea..."

The mattress dipped when he joined her. Before she could get used to the idea of his naked body hip to hip with hers, he dragged her beneath him and began to suckle her breasts one at a time. The fiery pleasure spun from her nipples to her womb, rekindling hot, shivering need.

His hips pinned her down, effectively making her a prisoner. But with his erection trapped between them, the kind of release she wanted would only come from his body entering hers. Almost sobbing in frustration, she grabbed fistfuls of his hair and guided his mouth to hers. "Kiss me, Pierce. Kiss me again."

She loved the way he did it, lazy dueling tongues, sharp

nips at her top lip, slow, steady torture when he took her bottom lip between his teeth and pulled gently.

Finally, it was too much. She arched her back and wriggled and scooted. But it was no use. Pierce was in control of the timetable.

"Please," she begged. "Don't make us wait. I can't stand it."

He looked down at her, a lock of hair falling onto his forehead. Sweat dampened his brow. His scent was something wonderful, a mélange of plain shower soap and piney aftershave and warm aroused male. Even with his cheekbones darkened with color, his gaze was teasing. "I kind of like having you in my power."

"Neanderthal." There wasn't much heat in her accusation. It was hard to criticize a man so dedicated to giving pleasure.

"I could play with your body for hours," he murmured, smoothing a strand of hair from her face. "But if I don't have you soon, I may spontaneously combust."

"Well, we wouldn't want that." She kissed his nose and his chin and his hard shoulder. "I'm ready when you are."

From the look on his face, it pained him to leave her, but he moved away just long enough to retrieve one of the condoms he'd tossed on the nightstand. Rolling it into place, he faced her once more, stretched out on his side. "Thank you for coming with me today." The expression in his eyes was the most open she'd ever seen from him.

She knew his statement was dead serious, and it made her want to cry. So she covered up her emotions with a quip. "Thank you for making me come."

He stared at her, lips curled in a smile that resembled a pirate about to plunder and pillage. "Don't thank me yet. You can roll them all into one."

Again, he covered her body with his, only now he aligned them for practicality. Taking both of her wrists in one big hand, he held her arms over her head. "You're pushy and stubborn and sometimes aggravating as hell, and I need you more than any woman I've ever known. Close your eyes, Nikki. I want you to feel us."

She did as he asked, and lost all the oxygen from her lungs when she felt the inexorable push of his possession. Big and fully aroused, he managed only an inch or so at first.

He kissed her cheek. "Relax, honey."

She tried, she really did. But every nerve in her body was rigged to a timer set to explode, and she couldn't seem to catch her breath. He rocked back and forth…back and forth, gaining new ground with each slide. Skin on skin. Heart to heart. Arching her back, she gained him another few centimeters. Unbearably full, uncomfortably stretched, she panted. With her vision wiped out, the universe pinwheeled, little flashes of light pulsing in time with his thrusts.

Something coiled strong and hot, low in her belly. She squeezed her inner muscles and heard him curse. No longer able to bear the dark, she opened her eyes and saw his face. He was a man at the edge, trying with all his might to hold on.

Deliberately, she dug her fingernails into his shoulders. "Finish it, Pierce. I need all of you."

His gaze went blank. A mighty shudder racked his frame. He bowed his head and then reared back with a muffled shout as his hips pistoned.

She wanted to be there with him at the end, but she had been too close for too long. With a helpless cry, her hips ground into his and she felt the scalding heat of a climax so intense, she lost a few seconds in the aftermath.

Dimly, she heard Pierce groan as he came. His body went lax and heavy on hers. Exhaustion claimed her, and she slept....

Pierce awoke disoriented. Several things came back to him all at once. Nikki. Hot, sweaty sex. Feeling himself turned inside out by her generous passion. He lay still for a moment, cataloging the situation. She was curled against his side, one arm across his chest, one leg resting on his thigh.

He craned his neck to see the clock. Only seven-thirty, and it felt like midnight. A responsible man would call the hospital. But at the moment, he reveled in selfishness...savored the sheer perfection of having Nicola Parrish in his bed. He'd known from the first moment that she flipped his switches. But *good God almighty,* she was amazing.

Even now, his spent erection was springing to life. "Nikki?" He shook her arm gently.

"Hmm?" She opened her eyes sleepily, and for a moment he saw shock.

"You're not dreaming," he said smugly. "Yes, I did rock your world."

She yawned. "If I had the energy, I'd slap you for that."

"Kinky, but I'm game." He grabbed another condom, donned it and rolled her to her side, facing away from him. "Go back to sleep," he said, only half kidding. "I may be done with you in another three or eight or seventeen hours." The way he felt right now, he could take her again and again until the sun rose.

Lifting her leg and draping it over his thigh, he entered her from behind, feeling the unfamiliar squeeze of a new angle. With her breast cupped in his hand, he moved slowly, deliberately. The edge of his hunger was blunted for the moment by his earlier release. But like a flame to dry wood, the feel of her body in his embrace caught him up in a new conflagration.

He shaped her breast in his palm, pinching lightly at the nipple. Nikki made a noise that indicated approval. Her bottom nestled closer, deepening penetration. He licked the top of her spine, incredibly aroused by the vulnerability of her nape.

Suddenly, all he could see was a quiet, lost teenager. The image broke his heart. His movements slowed, and he kissed her again...her shoulder, the tiny indentations in her spine. Her sunlit hair.

Moving carefully so as not to break the connection, he rolled to his back, keeping her on top of him as he pushed her into a seated position.

She glanced over her shoulder with a wary, questioning gaze. But she didn't speak.

He grasped her butt and thrust upward. "Take it where you want to go, Nikki. I'm all yours."

The new position seemed to stymie her for a half second. But she quickly adjusted, putting her hands on his knees and leaning forward so she could lift and lower herself onto him. The curve of her waist mesmerized him, as did the smooth, pale heart shape of her rear.

Thinking the more shallow penetration would allow him to last longer was a severe miscalculation. When Nikki cried out in release, the peak rushed at him out of nowhere. He disengaged their bodies only long enough to reposition her and then shuddered helplessly as he thrust repeatedly into her tight, warm passage and exploded in a wave of pleasure that seemed endless.

Some time later, he felt Nikki stir. She left the bed, and he was aware that the bathroom light turned on. Half dozing, he heard water running. And then noted the almost silent pad of her feet on the carpet as she came back to him.

Her limbs were chilled from the air conditioning. He pulled her close and closed his eyes. The only peace he had known since the doctor told him he was not a donor match was right here in this bed.

The drapes were closed. A sliver of sunlight told him that the summer evening was far from over.

Nikki played with the hair on his arm. "Are you going to the hospital?"

"For ten minutes? Knowing that my presence might give her a heart attack? I don't think so. We'll regroup in the morning."

Nikki picked up his hand and kissed it, brushing her lips over his knuckles. "It's going to be okay…I promise."

Ten

Nikki awoke before dawn, her eyes gritty from lack of sleep. She and Pierce had made love for most of the night, only pausing around 1:00 a.m. for another call to room service. Pierce had been insatiable, taking her over and over in every position imaginable, including one memorable coupling where he pressed her against the window of their upper-floor hotel room.

The fee for her lodging had been a complete waste—Pierce flatly refused to let her go back to her room. Sometime after four they had fallen into an exhausted slumber, their arms and legs twined together as if they couldn't bear to be separated. It was true enough on her part. Pierce had sneaked into her heart and set up his tent.

At the moment he was sleeping like the dead. She slipped quietly out of bed and returned to her own room via the connecting door. After a quick shower, she blew dry her hair and changed into another of her business suits, this one a summer-weight gray jacket and skirt. She paired it with a fuchsia blouse that normally cheered her with its hot splash of color.

Today it might take more than a blouse. Though she was giddy about her feelings for Pierce, she forced herself to tuck them away. She needed to be strong for him today. *He* needed her to take the lead in this investigation, even if he didn't know it. Aunt Gertrude was frail and ill. If she died without providing the answers they needed, Pierce might never get over it. So Nikki would do what had to be done.

When she was fully dressed, she reloaded her suitcase so it would be ready when and if they checked out. Neither of them had brought much in the way of spare clothes, so if this trip dragged on, they would have to regroup.

Glancing around the room, she checked to make sure she hadn't forgotten anything. Then, quietly, she stepped back through the connecting door. Seeing Pierce sprawled in the bed, his beautiful chest rising and falling with steady breathing, twisted something inside her. She wanted to photograph *him*...the bed...the room. Anything to preserve the memory of one incredible night.

But instead of climbing beneath the covers and awakening him with a kiss, she had to play bad cop. It was a role she did not relish. Everything about what she was about to do broke her heart. But for Pierce, she would put aside her own personal inclinations and give him the help he had asked for in the beginning.

When her chin wobbled and her throat burned, she blinked back the tears. Touching his foot beneath the blanket, she shook it gently. "Wake up, Pierce. It's time to go back to the hospital."

His head moved from side to side, a frown creasing his forehead. Gradually he opened his eyes and looked around him. "Nikki?"

She gave him a small smile. "Yes. I know you're tired, but we have to go. I called and checked on Gertrude. She's stable and they've moved her to a room."

Running a hand through his hair, he cursed. "I don't want to go to the hospital. I want you back in this bed where you belong."

Seeing him all sleep rumpled and gorgeous tested her resolve. But he had hired her to find answers, and her job was to make sure that happened. "Get up, Pierce. We had our fun last night. Now it's back to the real world. I'll order some breakfast while you're in the shower."

Anger darkened his face. "What in the hell is wrong with you?"

"Nothing," she said simply. "We came here to talk to your aunt. That's what we're going to do. I think I should go in first and test the waters. If I can get her to admit she knows something, I'll insist that you come in to hear what she has to say. I know how to deal with the elderly. You don't have to worry that I'll upset her."

He crawled out of bed and stretched, apparently unfazed by his nudity in her presence. She, on the other hand, had to look away. No man should be allowed to have such physical beauty. It wasn't fair to the female sex.

When he put his hands on his hips, she realized he was taunting her. "I feel a little cheap," he said with what came close to being a sneer. "I thought women liked to snuggle."

"Pierce…" She hesitated, unsure what to say. Could she tell him that he was the most amazing man she'd ever met? That she was halfway in love with him already? That if she could have anyone, it would be him?

No. That's not what he needed to hear. Not today. Today he needed the bossy lawyer, not the sexual playmate. Today was important. Today could change his life.

She made herself go to him, touching him on the arm with an apologetic smile. "I'd rather go back to bed with you…I would. But you can't shut this out, no matter how much it upsets you. It's better to know what you're facing than to always wonder."

"How can you be so sure?" The words were raw...stark... and his face was a study in torment.

"Because I know what it is to live without those answers, and I wouldn't wish that misery on anyone."

He stared at her for long, heated seconds before his shoulders dropped and he spun on his heel to head to the shower.

She hadn't realized she'd been holding her breath, but relief whooshed out in a loud sigh, making her light-headed. Neither of them was in any shape for an emotional gauntlet, but they would do what they had to do, because they had no choice.

It was nine o'clock when they pulled into the hospital parking lot. Pierce was driving this time. He was dressed in a crisply starched blue shirt and black trousers. It occurred to her that she had never seen him in any of his outdoor gear. He had said he wanted to teach her how to kick back and relax, but circumstances had led them in a different direction.

Once inside, they visited the gift shop and then found the waiting room on the appropriate floor. Pierce was like a nervous jungle animal. He couldn't sit, despite her cajoling. "Go," he said. "See what you can find out."

She went up on tiptoe and kissed his cheek. "I'll text you if I think she's ready to talk."

Nikki was projecting more confidence than she actually felt. If Gertrude clammed up, there was no guarantee that Nikki or anyone else could get her to talk. If she had secrets, she'd kept them for over three decades. That was a long time to protect the past. And as old as she was, the elderly woman might simply decide to take her secrets to the grave.

The door to the room was ajar. Nikki stood for a moment, listening to see if a nurse or doctor was inside. At last, she tiptoed in. Pierce's great-aunt was dozing. In a hospital gown, with her skin sallow and her hair unbrushed, she looked even older than she had in the nursing home.

Nikki sat down in a chair at the foot of the bed and positioned it so that she would be immediately visible when the patient roused. Though it might have been okay, she couldn't bring herself to awaken Gertrude. Not with what had happened yesterday. She hoped to keep things unthreatening and low key.

Suddenly, out in the hallway, someone dropped what sounded like a meal tray. The noise was loud enough to wake the dead. Gertrude's eyes snapped open. Immediately, she spotted Nikki. Though she winced when she recognized her visitor, her gaze was alert.

Her mouth worked as she reached for a water carafe. "You're Pierce's friend."

Nikki jumped up to help her with the drink. "Yes, ma'am. I'm Nikki Parrish. I brought you those flowers." She had placed the vase of pink roses and baby's breath on the rolling table beside the bed.

"Where's the boy?"

"Down the hall. He had a business call to make, but he'll be along shortly." It was a feeble lie, but for the moment, necessary.

"Never kid a kidder, honey. He's scared he'll make me keel over again."

Nikki shrugged. "Maybe. What did the doctor say?"

"It could be any number of things at my age…a piece of plaque breaking off, a tiny clot somewhere…"

"Or an anxiety attack?"

Gertrude's bark of laughter was hoarse. "You don't mess around do you, darlin'? Yes, of course. It could have been an anxiety attack. You forget that I'm a physician. I may not have practiced medicine for lo these many years, but I remember enough to know that when the body gets to be ninety-two, any one of a number of things can bring it down."

"How are you feeling this morning?"

"Old. Sad. Guilty." She stared at Nikki with a bleak twist of her lips. "He knows, doesn't he?"

Nikki pulled her chair closer. "Only that he's not who he thought he was. But that's all. I'm thinking you can help him with the rest. Please, Miss Gertrude. He's a mess. Promise me you'll tell him what you know."

"He won't like what I have to say."

"I didn't really think he would. But he deserves the truth, don't you think?"

"How did he find out?"

"You know his father is very ill."

"Yes. My niece has talked to me about it often."

"Pierce decided he wanted to be the one to donate a kidney to his dad if he was a match."

Gertrude sank down in the bed, pulling the sheet to her chin. Her eyes glistened with tears. "God save us all. They told him he wasn't related."

"Yes, ma'am. Can you even imagine what that did to him?" Nikki felt like a bitch for interrogating an old, sick woman, but what choice did she have? "He and his mother are devastated."

"And his father?"

"They haven't told him yet, partly because he is so ill, and partly because they wanted to investigate and hopefully get some kind of explanation before they dropped that kind of bomb."

"I'm not a bad person."

"I don't know you, but Pierce told me what you did for his mother. How you took her in and raised her as your own child. I can't imagine you would do anything to hurt her, at least not intentionally."

"I would give my life for her. She and my daughter were all I had, and they are the best part of me."

"You devoted a great many years to your patients. That's no small matter. Medical care is personal and invaluable. I would imagine that you saved many lives and helped many people."

One wrinkled hand lifted to cover her eyes, her face ashen. "I abused my position...." Her voice was barely audible.

Nikki knew the time had come. "Shall I ask Pierce to join us now?" She kept the words firm and unemotional, though inside she was aching for what was to come.

Gertrude nodded, the slight movement of her head barely perceptible. "Yes. Tell him it's time."

Just as Nikki was texting Pierce, one of the nurses came in to check vital signs.

"I'll wait in the hall," Nikki said.

When Pierce walked up, she was leaning against the wall, her stomach churning with dread. "Hey there," she said. "The nurse is with her, but it will only be a minute."

Pierce's face was grim. "What did she tell you?"

"Not much. Only enough to let me know that your secret dates back to her."

He nodded jerkily. "Can she handle this? I don't want to kill her."

"She's old, but she's strong. And I think she wants to be done with it."

When the nurse walked out of the room, Pierce stopped the young woman. "How is she doing?"

"Are you family?"

"Yes...her nephew. Great-nephew, actually."

"She's stable. The doctor will be around to talk to you in about an hour or so."

Nikki linked her hand with Pierce's, feeling the long fingers, the calluses, the warm skin. "You're a strong, wonderful man. You can handle whatever happens."

He put his arms around her, pressing his face to her hair. "Will you think less of me if I tell you my knees are shaking?"

She could hear the tremor in his voice. Hugging him tightly, she stroked his back. "I will never change my opinion of you. You are the most amazing man I know."

He pulled back and pressed the heels of his hands to his eyes for a long moment. "Are we talking about last night?"

As an attempt at levity, it fell flat, but she applauded his effort. "It's always about sex with you men, isn't it?"

He kissed her forehead and pulled back to look into her eyes, his own gaze intense. "I needed you last night and you were there," he said, the words rough and low. "I don't think you'll ever know how much that means to me." He brushed his thumb across her lower lip, sending tingles of remembered bliss echoing in her womb.

She swallowed back the emotion that threatened to drown her. "I'm here for as long as you need me. I won't leave you to face this alone."

He took a deep breath, his grip almost crushing the bones in her hand. "I'm ready."

Eleven

Pierce had experienced many physically harrowing moments in his life: being trapped upside down in a kayak when it wedged between two rocks…having to rescue a climber with hysteria who'd nearly killed them both on the side of a cliff…realizing that the snake he'd been bitten by was a rattler and he was fifteen miles from the nearest help.

He had always considered himself resourceful and levelheaded, able to keep calm in a crisis. But nothing had prepared him for this bone-deep dread that filled his veins with ice water.

He heard Nikki close the door as they walked in. Interruptions were de rigueur in a hospital, but the morning meal was over, the nurse had been in and the doctor would be by later. If they were lucky, no one would bother them for the next half hour.

Nikki offered him the chair, but he couldn't sit. His great-aunt shot him one fearful look and then stared at her hands. Pierce leaned against the counter by the window.

Silence reigned for at least three minutes…or maybe it was three hours. Time had ceased to have meaning.

Nikki rescued them all. She stood on the opposite side of the bed and took one of Gertrude's hands in hers. "I know you're afraid. And I know this is hard. But we need you to help us. Please, Miss Trudie. Tell us what happened when Pierce was born."

The old woman trembled visibly. Nikki shot Pierce a concerned glance, but he ignored it, staring instead at the floor, hoping he wouldn't throw up. Finally, without prompting, Gertrude reached for a button and raised the head of the bed. When she was seated upright, she drank some water and wiped her mouth with the back of her hand.

Pierce jerked when she spoke, his head snapping up in amazement at how strong her voice sounded.

Gertrude's words were slow, but distinct. "I love your mother perhaps more than I should. My own daughter and I had our differences, but from the moment I took home a beautiful little four-year-old girl, my life was the richer for it. Because of my divorce, I knew I would never have any more children of my own, so now I had two wonderful daughters."

Nikki had stepped back, but she prompted the dialogue. "What was the age difference in the two girls?"

"Five years. My Tessa was nine when I moved us lock, stock and barrel to Charlottesville. Though I didn't realize it at the time, she resented the upheaval, and even worse, she resented having her position as an only child usurped. By the time she was in high school, she had matured enough to love her little cousin, but it took a long time. And even though all of that is water under the bridge, Tessa occasionally exhibited traces of jealousy, even in the last years before she died."

"Was Tessa involved in any of what you're about to tell us?"

Pierce had a sudden vision of Nikki in a courtroom,

carefully examining the witness. Her questions were right on target.

Gertrude shook her head. "Not at all. But what I'm trying to explain is that my relationship with your mother was pure love. There were no hidden currents, no typical mother/daughter battles. She was affectionate and grateful and I adored her."

"Enough to commit a crime for her?" Pierce took a shot in the dark, and it hit its mark. Gertrude gaped and paled. He tasted bile. His stomach curled. Surely his aunt hadn't stolen a baby.

The old woman drank more water, and the room seemed to shrink as her story paused midstream. Finally, she spoke again. "I took an oath to do no harm," she said wearily. "But there are moments in life when circumstances convene to create unbearable choices. I don't think they ever told you, Pierce, but your parents thought they were unable to conceive. I loaned them tens of thousands of dollars for fertility treatments. But that was a long time ago, and the technology was not what it is now. Month after month, year after year, your dear mother tried and failed to get pregnant."

He shook his head. "No. They never told me."

"That kind of stress puts a strain on even the best of marriages. Your mother was distraught. Your father wanted to quit trying. They ended up in counseling, and then a miracle happened. She missed a period, had a pregnancy test and the celebrating began. You have no idea how euphoric they were. As a gift to the new child, I told them I didn't want a penny of the money returned. It had been worth every check I wrote to see their faces, and I knew I would have more than enough money to leave Tessa when I was gone."

So far the narrative seemed harmless. But Pierce knew there was more. "Was the pregnancy difficult?"

"Not at all. Your mother had been extremely careful with

her health. I recommended the best ob-gyn at our hospital to care for her. Everything was perfect. The pregnancy and delivery were textbook. The only complicating factor was the story you've heard many times."

"About the flu epidemic?"

"Yes. It decimated the hospital staff. In addition to having every bed filled, we were working at less than half capacity when it came to personnel. The night your mother went into labor, her doctor was at home with a temperature of a hundred and four degrees. Your mother begged me to deliver the baby, and of course I agreed. It's hard to watch someone you love suffer through labor. Your mother had an almost superstitious aversion to any kind of medical assistance, so she opted for natural childbirth. She and your father had been to Lamaze classes. They were as prepared as two people can be who've never experienced birth."

"And there really were no complications?"

"Other than a long labor, typical for first moms—no. She and your father were exhausted, though, and in the wee hours of the morning, they decided to let the baby go to the nursery so they could get some rest. It's more common now for the baby to stay in the room with the mother the entire time, but back then, it was not at all unusual to send the baby out for hours at a time so new moms could have uninterrupted sleep."

He made himself ask the next question. "Were there other deliveries that night?"

His aunt stared at him, her expression unreadable. "Yes, two. And I delivered them as well…a set of twins born about an hour after I had been with your mother. There was one other baby in the nursery, a little girl who had been born two days before. She was scheduled to go home the following morning. Because our load was light, and because several of my nurses had been working double shifts, I sent two of them home to rest. That left only one nurse and myself, but we agreed we could handle things until morning as long as no other women were admitted in labor. If that had happened, we would have called for reinforcements, of course."

She stopped talking, and her hands jerked uncontrollably for several seconds. Pierce stepped forward. "Aunt Trudie? Do I need to call someone?"

Huge tears welled and overflowed and ran down her wrinkled cheeks. "No. Let me finish."

He was torn. This narrative was shredding him, nerve by nerve. What must it be doing to his aunt? He could stop her. Walk away. Let the past be the past. But his feet were like lead, his limbs unable to move. He was stretched on a rack of indecision, desperate to hear the end of the story, but equally desperate to flee from it.

Overwhelmed with compassion for her pain, he went to her and kissed her soft white hair. "Go on, then. So we can be done with this."

Gratitude shone in her rheumy eyes. But also a dull acceptance of what could not be changed.

He returned to his position at the window, shooting a glance at Nikki. Her cheeks were wet and the smile she gave him was lopsided at best. Even across the room, with the hospital bed between them, he felt the force of her caring and concern.

Gertrude resumed her tale. He tensed, knowing that the end was not far off.

She had a faraway look in her eyes, as if she had slipped into the past. "It was 3:00 a.m.," she said. "My nurse was weaving on her feet. All four babies were sleeping. I told her to go into one of the empty rooms across the hall and close her eyes for an hour. I was hyped up on coffee and exhilaration for your parents.

"Hospitals are seldom quiet, but that night, for one brief period, peace reigned. Seeing those precious children filled me with such deep joy. This was why I had defied my own parents and gone into medicine. Even though my independent ways had cost me my marriage, it was all worth it.

"I checked the infants every fifteen minutes, particularly the newborns. But about four o'clock, one of them wasn't breathing."

Goddamn it. Pierce could barely force words from his throat. "Which one? Tell me which one."

"Your mother's child."

Everything in the room went black and there was a terrible roaring in his head. She didn't say, *you, Pierce.* Duh. He was standing here alive and well. She said, *your mother's child.* Not him. It had never been him. He was not an Avery.

An infinite, terrifying fury welled in his chest. "What did you do, old woman? What in God's name did you do?"

He barely noticed Nikki's gasp of consternation.

Gertrude seemed barely breathing, her skin sallow, her cheeks sunken. "I did CPR. I was completely cool and calm. I knew the procedures. Knew exactly what I had to do. But the baby was dead. Already turning cold. I was going to have to walk down that hall, awaken your parents, and tell them that this precious child they had wanted so desperately was gone. But I couldn't do it. I could not do it. Later, I realized that I was in shock, but at that moment, my mind seemed crystal clear. The couple in the room next to your mother's had given birth to twins. They hadn't even known they were expecting twins. We didn't do ultrasounds back then, and it wasn't all that uncommon for one twin to hide behind the other, meaning only one heartbeat was audible."

Pierce shook his head. "No, no, no..." This was some macabre horror movie, a terrible fiction.

She continued in a monotone. "I asked myself…why should they have two healthy babies and your parents none? I looked at the lab work. The blood types were different, so I knew the boys were fraternal twins. It was all done in an instant. I switched the babies in the bassinets, typed up two new bracelets to replace the ones I had to cut off, and it was finished. I summoned help per hospital procedure, and the chaplain went in to see the family who had lost a child."

"Not my parents…"

"No. Their baby was alive and well. In the coming days, the hospital performed an autopsy as was policy in these situations. Your mother's boy had been born with an irreversible heart defect. He could have actually died in the womb, but as it was, he lived for about six hours."

Pierce felt himself coming apart. In his head, he was taking Gertrude's neck in his two big hands and choking her until the life was gone. The vision was so real it terrified him. He didn't even know how badly he was shaking until he felt Nikki's arms around him.

She squeezed him tightly, murmuring to him, pressing her face to his chest.

He returned the embrace automatically, unable to process what was happening. His mother adored this wicked old hag and Pierce wanted to kill her. He shuddered. No, that wasn't true. He wasn't that kind of man. But these feelings of anguish, God, these feelings. How could he go forward from here? What did he do with this information? Good God in heaven, what choice did he have?

Suddenly, it dawned on him that the most important question had yet to be answered. He shook the bed rail angrily, startling Gertrude. "Who are my parents?" he yelled. "Who are they?"

His aunt blinked once…twice…and she wet her lips. "Vincent and Delores Wolff."

* * *

Nikki saw Pierce's face and knew he was beyond logical reasoning. She took his arm. "We need to go now. We'll come back when you've had some time to think this through."

He flung off her hand. "I'm not coming back," Pierce said, his tone incredulous. "Why would I subject myself to more of this?" His pupils were dilated and he was dragging in deep breaths and exhaling as if he had been running a marathon.

It was a toss-up as to who looked worse, Pierce or his great-aunt. Gertrude had slumped sideways against the pillows, and though she was breathing steadily, she didn't appear to know where she was.

Nikki coaxed him toward the door. "We're going back to the hotel," she said, infusing her voice with authority. "Come with me."

That he followed her was a surprise, but he had withdrawn to a place where nothing in the real world impinged on his consciousness. She led him like he was a blind man, steering him into and out of elevators and praying he wouldn't make a scene while they were in a public building.

She was worried about Gertrude, but the woman was hooked up to monitors, so surely someone would notice if she was having difficulties.

Once they reached the car, Nikki took the keys from Pierce's pocket and made him get in on the passenger's side. When they arrived at the hotel, front desk personnel looked at them oddly, but no one interrupted their progress.

One more elevator ride, and then finally, they were back at Pierce's door. "Give me your billfold," she said. When he stared at her blankly, she dug in her purse for her own key card, opened the door and went through to Pierce's room from her side.

She pushed him into a chair and poured him a glass of water. He was sweating, and his skin looked gray beneath his tan. "What am I going to tell them?" he asked, his tone desolate. "How do I tell them their baby died?"

Nikki crouched in front of him, her hands on his knees. "You're still their son, Pierce. They are not losing you. They are *not* losing you."

Her words made no apparent dent in the haze of pain that engulfed him. Her own throat ached from the effort to hold back tears. Feeling helpless and alone and totally unprepared to do anything to ease his misery, she found herself pacing the room while he sat, statuelike, where she had placed him.

When her legs grew tired, she sat on a chair opposite him. After an hour passed, she spoke softly to him until he followed her to the bed. She folded back the covers and made him lie down. Putting out the do not disturb sign and drawing the drapes, she curled up beside him and slept.

Pierce opened his eyes and stared at the ceiling. His chest hurt, and his head felt oddly empty. He couldn't remember where he was, and that alarmed him so much, he sat up in the bed. Then he saw her...Nikki. And everything came flooding back. A howl of agony rose in his lungs, his throat, but he clamped his teeth shut to keep it in. Already he had made a fool of himself in front of Nikki. She'd handled him like a baby when he had checked out of reality for a time.

He felt physically sluggish and mentally slow, as if he had been in a car accident and suffered a head injury. That had happened to him once. He'd been unconscious for almost two days. His parents had kept a vigil by his bedside until he awoke. His parents. The man and woman who raised him. But no, they were not his parents. Their baby died.

Feeling for some point of human contact, he took Nikki's free hand. The other one was tucked beneath her cheek as she slept. Still dressed in what she had worn to the hospital, she looked exhausted and not at all comfortable.

Pierce held her hand in the semi-dark room and tried to make a plan. He was a grown man. Used to being in charge of a business. Accustomed to making decisions and looking out for multiple groups of people who trusted him to make sure their outdoor experiences were both safe and fun.

But it was as if someone had turned off a switch in his brain. What did he do now? Check out? Go home? He couldn't imagine returning to the hospital. The very thought of it filled him with revulsion. A compassionate person should be able to forgive an old woman for an ancient wrongdoing. But he couldn't. He wouldn't. Some sins were too heinous for absolution.

Gradually, one thing became clear to him. Even if he was the proverbial rudderless ship in a storm, he was not going to drag Nikki down with him. And he was not going to be some pathetic figure who needed hand-holding and TLC. He was a man. And it was about time he started acting like one.

It took every ounce of mental fortitude he could muster to make himself get out of bed, grab a couple of things from his suitcase and stumble into the bathroom. He closed the door quietly, not wanting to wake Nikki. Every time she looked at him with those big, liquid blue eyes, he felt naked and raw, and he couldn't deal with that now.

In the shower, he turned the dial to just below scalding, trying to wash away the stench of hospital smells and the memories that clung to him like cobwebs. *Out, out damned spot.* Shakespeare knew a thing or two about this condition. And the need to purge the past. The hot water was restorative, but no matter how long he stood beneath the spray, his insides were cold.

The only other clean shirt he'd brought was a cheery yellow with a blue stripe. He winced, seeing himself in the mirror. Funeral clothing would have been more appropriate. Somber and dark to match his mood.

He cut himself shaving. His hands couldn't seem to hold the razor steady. But finally, he was finished. He was ready. The first thing on his list could be checked off. *Get out of bed and pretend like you're in charge.*

Perhaps if he acted out the fiction long enough, it would begin to be true.

When he returned to the bedroom, Nikki was still asleep. He sat in a chair and watched her. With no place to go and no particular timetable, he wasn't in a hurry to face the remainder of the day. So he sat in the dark and brooded. Gradually, memories of his aunt's halting narrative began to be replaced by memories of the night before.

Nikki's face alight with laughter. Nikki, eyes closed, hands clenched in the sheets as he made her come. Nikki, calling out his name as he entered her and moved inside her. Given her past, it was a miracle she was not an embittered woman. Instead, she was generous to a fault with her emotions and her passion.

The thought that she might be moving away from him in a few weeks was a sharp spike to the heart. She had come into his life when he was at his weakest moment. Though he had not always deserved it, she'd given him empathy, sympathy and the benefit of her wisdom and experience.

He knew, sitting here in this dark, anonymous hotel room, that she was the kind of woman with whom he could make a life. But Nikki had strong ideas about things, and Pierce knew instinctively that she would expect him to follow a path he wasn't prepared to tread.

Physically, Pierce was prepared for any challenge. He was at the peak of his capabilities. His body was in perfect condition. Heart rate, muscle mass, endurance. Whatever life threw at him, whether it was negotiating a river, climbing a mountain or trekking on foot through the wilderness, he was ready.

But not for this. Never for this. He was angry and confused and hurt. Unfortunately, he couldn't let Nikki see the extent of his crippling mental turmoil. She'd want to help him and fix him and save him, and that was unacceptable. A man was supposed to clear his own trail.

It was a long time before she woke up. By then he was actually beginning to feel hungry. She sat up and stared at him, her gaze wary. "Are you okay?" she asked, clearly thinking he wasn't.

He shrugged. "Okay enough. If you don't mind, as soon as you've had a chance to freshen up, I'd like to check out and head home. We can grab something to eat on the way."

Confusion colored her face. "But what about the hospital?"

"No need to go back. We got what we came for. I need to check in at work."

"You said your assistant manager had things covered."

"Doesn't mean I'm not still the boss."

"And Gertrude?"

He heard the unspoken questions, but ignored them. "She's receiving excellent care. No reason for us to hang around."

"But—"

He held up his hand. "I'm starving, Nikki. Let's get out of here."

In forty-five minutes they were in his car headed back to Charlottesville. He was driving. Nikki sat beside him in silence. He got the impression she was afraid to talk to him in case he had a breakdown. Insulting, perhaps, but possibly on target.

After deciding to drive through a fast-food place, they ate burgers in the car. With the radio playing softly, the miles flew past. Nikki had shed her jacket and was playing with the bow on her silky blouse. She had kicked off her shoes as well.

He turned his head briefly, managing a smile. "You don't have to be afraid of me. My Jekyll and Hyde performance is over."

"I'd never be afraid of you, Pierce. You have a right to be upset."

"Well, I'm fine now, so no worries."

Her expression was dubious, but he would convince her. All he had to do was act as if everything was normal. And actually, nothing had really changed. His dad was still sick. That was the crux of the matter.

Nikki surprised him, though. She cut to the chase with a question he hadn't expected. "So when are you going to contact the Wolffs?"

Controlling his inner rage, he kept his words even and without inflection. "I'm not."

"But you have to, Pierce," she said urgently. "They need to know what happened. They need to know that you're alive."

"Sorry to disappoint you, but no. In the first place, I don't give a damn about the Wolffs, and in the second place, can you imagine their reaction if a 'long-lost son' showed up on their doorstep? Give me some credit. I'm not going to live my life like some soap opera where the dead come to life whenever the ratings need a boost."

"They're your family," she said, sounding as if she might cry.

"No. They're not. And perhaps you haven't thought of one other very real possibility. What do you think they might do to a woman who kidnapped their child and gave it away? Send her to prison? Humiliate her in front of the world? Sue her and take everything she has?"

"Oh."

"Yeah. *Oh* is right. Gertrude is not going to tell anyone what she knows. And I sure as hell am not. So unless you can't keep a secret, this thing is dead, pardon the pun."

"But what are you going to tell your mother?"

His gut churned. He'd been thinking about that ad nauseam, and he knew that to protect his mom he had to keep his mouth shut, even if the truth would be cathartic and healing for Pierce. "I'll tell her the medical records showed nothing out of the ordinary and that Gertrude didn't remember anything either. Why would I torture my mother when she has so much to handle as it is? That night long ago is over. Done with. I'm going on with my life."

Twelve

Nikki ached for Pierce. She knew instinctively that he was making a dreadful mistake. Secrets were never a good thing. If he kept this knowledge to himself, he would suffer deeply.

No matter how much she wanted to advise him, she had no right to do so. This was not a legal matter. It was deeply personal, and he had made up his mind.

Shock was still guiding his actions. Surely she would be able to get through to him after a day or two. In the meantime, perhaps he could use some space. Men tended to lick their wounds in private. But on the other hand, she wasn't sure he should be alone. At least not yet.

As they reached the suburbs of Charlottesville, she took a breath. What could she say? *Thanks for taking me with you? I had a good time?*

She cleared her throat. "Would you like to come up to my place and stay for a while? We can pop popcorn…watch old movies."

Some of the tension left his body, because she saw his shoulders sag. "Actually," he said, his voice hoarse, "I'd like that very much."

In minutes he parked in front of her building and they took the elevator to her floor. Her condo was hot because she had turned the air off when she left. She kicked up the AC, handed Pierce the remote and excused herself to go change clothes. As she stepped naked into the shower, visions of last night played in her brain. Despite the trauma of the morning, she couldn't forget the hours she and Pierce had spent together.

As the warm water pelted down on her shoulders, she felt some of her tension ease. Pierce needed time. And she, for once, was not on the clock, not counting every minute, worrying about the piles of work stacking up. Perhaps the best thing she could do was simply be there for him.

If he wanted sex, she would be happy. But if all he needed was companionship, that was okay, too.

She slipped on a comfy pair of yoga pants and a soft cotton top in lacy cream-colored voile. The blouse was lined with a second transparent layer, so she omitted a bra. Fastening thin gold hoops in her ears, she glanced in the mirror and smiled. She looked like a scruffy gypsy, but that was okay, because her lawyer persona was on trial for the next few weeks.

Now was the time for self-reflection…relaxation…and peace.

Pierce looked up when she entered the living room. He scanned her from head to toe with heat in his gaze. "You don't much like shoes, do you?"

She shook her head. "No. At the orphanage we were required to wear shoes all the time, even in summer. But they were always hand-me-downs, so they never fit correctly. We always had blisters and calluses. When I received my first paycheck at my first real job, I went out and bought a pair of hot-pink high heels. I only wore them around the house, but those shoes made me feel like *somebody*. I could have been a princess in those shoes. Even so, I'd just as soon go barefooted whenever possible."

"Come sit by me." He patted the sofa cushion.

"Do you want something to drink?" she asked, nervous now that they were alone. He looked big and gorgeous and dangerous sprawled on her couch with his sock-clad feet propped on her coffee table.

"Quit playing hostess and get over here." In his deliberately bossy command, he was teasing her. And a shadow of the playful Pierce reappeared.

Smiling, she did as he asked. His arm went around her as she curled up beside him. She leaned her head on his chest, feeling her heart break just a little bit. She knew at least some of the pain he was feeling. The sense of being adrift. But nothing she could say right now would make a difference. So she might as well carpe diem and enjoy her time with him.

Pierce, after that first greeting, appeared totally engrossed in the movie. It was an early Stallone film. Closing her eyes at one of the gorier parts, she let herself float on a cloud of pleasure. Even this simple contact was precious. Having Pierce in her home made her realize that she was going to have to work harder at creating a life for herself away from work. She didn't want to end up old and alone. And she wanted children....

Once she made this job decision, she would lay out some rules for the other parts of her life. Make more time for friends. Take more risks in dating. Put her past behind her and be defined by who she was now, not then.

It all sounded good. But she knew herself pretty well. If she took the position in D.C., she'd likely get sucked into a high-powered world of sixty-hour workweeks. Was that what she really wanted? It was darned flattering to be asked. But in the end, would it be a terrible mistake?

She shifted once, and Pierce must have thought she was getting ready to stand up, because his arm clamped around her. "Stay here." He had been playing with her hair, and the simple caress had aroused her.

Embarrassment heated her cheeks. Pierce had been through hell today. She was sure he didn't even remember their wild sex play the night before. Men lived in the moment when it came to carnal pursuits. *She* might be reliving every single second, but he was absorbed with the on-screen action.

The credits rolled and Pierce stretched, glancing at his watch. Suddenly, his face changed.

"What?" she asked. "What is it?"

"I'm supposed to be somewhere tonight…and it's important."

"Oh." Disappointment flooded her. Here she was hoping he might want to spend the night, and he was concerned about his social calendar. "Are you sure you're up for that?"

"Doesn't matter. I've agreed to present an award. It's a black-tie gala to benefit the Appalachian Trail Conservancy. Both of Virginia's senators and the governor are going to do a drive-by five-minute speech. And I'm on the board, so I have to be there." He stopped, cocked his head and grinned. A ghost of his usual grin, but a grin nevertheless. "You could come with me," he said.

"I wouldn't know what to wear."

"You can't tell me that somewhere in your closet you don't have one fancy dress."

He had her there. She'd been shopping with a friend in Atlanta after a law symposium back in the spring, and purely on impulse, had bought a dress at Neiman Marcus on the clearance rack for a fraction of the original price. It was black and made of a heavy jersey fabric covered in spangles and beads that felt deliciously comfortable and yet sexy when she walked.

"I suppose I might. But you don't have a ticket for me."

Pierce took her foot in his hand and began to massage it. Goose bumps broke out all over her body. He used his thumb on her arch. "Not to worry. I wrote them a check for ten thousand dollars this year. I think they'll make room. But if it will make you feel better, I'll send the director's admin a text."

Now his hands were on her ankle. The massage felt wonderful, but she squirmed, her body flooding with heat. "I think I'll go make a pot of coffee," she said, needing to calm down.

Pierce abandoned her leg and took her face in both of his hands. "Kiss me, Nikki." His eyes were clear, nothing but hunger in them. As if by sheer strength of will he had put all else aside to concentrate on her.

She put everything she had into the kiss, everything he wouldn't let her say. Her sympathy, her heartbreak for him, the echoes of her own sad childhood. For long moments, that was enough. His tenderness wrapped around her heart and warmed her, making her believe that nothing else in his universe was as important as this kiss.

Finally, when her lips felt puffy and her neck ached from the angle, he released her…sat back…and grimaced. "I'm having a hard time telling you what I want. But at the risk of sounding crass, I want *you,* Nikki. More than you can imagine. More than is sane. I need to lose myself in you."

She sank her teeth into her bottom lip, telling herself she wouldn't cry. If nothing else, she could offer him physical release. Pleasure upon pleasure to help him forget. Boldly, she placed a hand on his leg. "I think that can be arranged. But my bed's pretty small, not even close to a king size."

He slid a hand under her hair and kissed her neck just below her ear. "Doesn't really matter. I don't plan to let you get that far away."

Pierce let her lead him down the hallway, feeling the twin pulls of shame and desire. He didn't want her to think he was using her, but he was...in a way. During the two-hour movie, he had been incredibly aware of her sitting against him. He'd inhaled her light flowery scent, had noted the way she breathed and had listened to the engaging sound of her laughter when she made fun of some stupid line of macho dialogue.

Her simple presence had helped him calm down. Nothing had changed. His life was still a shambles. But with Nikki, he found that he could put all that aside for a moment and simply *be*.

Her bedroom was revealing. Nothing of the buttoned-up lawyer at all. To say her furnishings were eclectic was an understatement. It looked as if she had raided the yard sale of a mad wizard and his fairy sprites. Everything was beaded and colorful, from a lopsided ottoman in turquoise and orange to lampshades fringed in multicolored beads.

The comforter was red silk, embroidered with vibrantly colored hummingbirds. And the walls were painted a pale celery green that somehow managed to draw everything together into harmony.

Nikki leaned against the wall, a half smile on her face. "Not what you were expecting, is it?"

He shrugged, still looking around. On the dresser sat a blown-glass mushroom. The central light fixture was a small antique chandelier. Beneath his feet lay an incredibly old Oriental rug, the colors faded with time and the occasional bare spot noticeable. But it was the real deal, not a fake.

Shoving his hands in his pockets, he grinned. "I like it, but yes, you've managed to surprise me. I feel like I should be smoking pot and weaving daisy chains."

"Bite your tongue, Pierce Avery. I uphold the law, so don't get any ideas."

He watched as she carefully folded back the covers. When she paused to look over her shoulder, she caught him staring at her curvy ass.

"If you're going to bend over like that, don't blame me," he said.

With what appeared to be deliberate movements, she stripped off her Lycra pants, now wearing only a sheer blouse and tiny panties. In the midst of this crazy room, she looked right at home. She held out her hand. "Let me give you the tour," she whispered. The husky note in her voice gave him hope that she was at least a fraction as wound up as he was. Last night had been beyond words. And now, new madness beckoned.

He watched, dry mouthed, as Nikki sat down on the side of the bed and waited for him to join her. His feet were glued to the floor, because he was inches away from taking her without ceremony. His fists clenched, he tried to steady his breathing. "Why all the color?" he asked, hoping to distract himself.

A shadow crossed her face, but she answered him. "At the home, there *was* no color. Institutional beige on the walls. Well-scarred wooden floors. Thin brown bedspreads. Even the curtains on the windows were an odd bisque color. One year at Christmas a local church gave every child in the orphanage a box of a hundred and twenty-eight Crayola crayons. I cried when I opened it, because I found all the colors that had been taken away. Later, when I was out on my own, I understood about trying to fit in and being conventional, but I decided that my bedroom was my private space, and if I wanted to run amok with palettes, it was my choice."

Again, she had done it to him. Made his throat burn with helpless emotion for the little girl who had no one. And she wasn't angling for sympathy. He had asked a question, and she had answered.

Tenderness sneaked in, tempering the driving need he felt. "Thank you for inviting me in," he said. "I hope I can live up to your color scheme. It's full of life and energy and passion. I like it."

He could see in her eyes that she was pleased by his response. And it made him wonder if another man had ever tried to squelch her unconventional streak of whimsy.

Without ceremony, he stripped out of his clothes. Nikki's cheeks flushed, but she didn't look away. When he was nude, a thought struck him. "I only have one condom left."

"I think that's all you have time for, Mr. Hotshot. If I'm going to the ball tonight, Cinderella needs a little time to get ready."

"Fair point."

He stood in front of her, smoothing her hair, playing with her ears. Gently, he lifted the hem of her blouse and pulled it over her head. He'd known she wasn't wearing a bra. Guys noticed. But seeing her like this made his heart stop. Last night he'd thought he had studied every inch of her. Something about this feminine room framed her in a new way. He saw her playful side and was enchanted.

He wasn't prepared when she took his shaft between her hands and warmed it. His knees locked. "Careful, Nikki. I might be a tad too primed."

"From watching a Stallone movie?" She tasted the head of his erection, swirling her tongue around it until he was dizzy.

"No, damn it. From holding you for two hours. A guy

can only take so much foreplay. You're lucky I didn't do you on the coffee table."

Her pleased giggle made him smile, even though every nerve in his body was raw and fiery.

"You're a beautiful man, Pierce Avery." She took him into her mouth and he cursed. It was all he could do to hold back his completion. Just when he thought he couldn't stand another second, she scooted back to the center of the mattress, making room for him.

Half crippled with desire, he pulled her into his arms and spooned her, telling himself he could hold out a bit longer.

Nikki sighed, a long, dreamy exhalation. "A man who cuddles…do I have to pay extra for this?"

He bit the back of her neck in response to her sass. "I'll have you know I'm exhibiting phenomenal restraint."

"I can tell."

His erection was pressed up against her butt. And when she deliberately wiggled her firm, soft fanny, he groaned. "You're a tease," he said gruffly.

"Should I stop?" She covered his hand with hers where it gripped her breast.

"I'm sorry," he said.

"For what?"

Somehow this confession was easier since she couldn't see his face. "I'm sorry you had to be there today."

He felt her go still. "It's okay."

"I was afraid it might have made you think of things you've gotten past. Like who was there when you were born."

She lifted his hand to her lips and kissed it. "I'll never get past it, Pierce. Not really. But I've adjusted to a new reality."

And you'll have to, as well. She didn't say the words out loud, but he heard them anyway. His brain rejected the thought. And chastised him for bringing up the taboo topic in the middle of Nikki's bed.

He let go of her and reached for the condom, donning it with shaky hands. "Do you trust me?" he asked.

She lay on her back, watching him, still wearing those sexy undies. "I do."

"Then take my hand."

Puzzlement crossed her face, but she did as he asked. Steadying her as they both got up and stood beside the bed, he caressed her breasts...one, and then the other. Nikki gasped, her nipples beading and her fair skin flushing as it did when she was excited. "If you're planning on picking me up, I'm not all that light."

"Another day," he promised. "I've been inspired by your decor."

She looked at him curiously, a tiny wrinkle appearing between her brows. "As in swinging from the chandelier?"

"Not that." He chuckled softly as he took her hand and led her to the ottoman. "I thought we'd try out this intriguing piece of furniture."

Thirteen

Nikki's expression was priceless. "Um…"

"You said you trust me."

"I do.…" Her eyes were big, as if what he was suggesting was wicked.

Come to think of it, the thoughts he was having definitely might fall under that category. "Then kneel for me, Nikki… on this oh-so-soft stool." The bright fabrics were satiny, and he had a hunch they would feel stimulating against her breasts.

She glanced down at his straining erection, her gaze a gratifying mixture of fascination, eagerness and trepidation. "I can do that."

Gracefully, she knelt, her hands resting on the cushion.

"All the way," he said. "Drape yourself over it."

He heard her breath catch. The audible evidence of her excitement made him tremble. As she obeyed his request, the additional visual stimulation was sheer torture for him. Breathing heavily, he went to his knees as well. Her pretty bottom was there before him, clad only in a few strips of white nylon and lace.

Moving forward, he spread his knees until his thighs pressed against the backs of hers. With long, firm strokes, he massaged her back, starting low on her spine and moving all the way up to her shoulders. Her head fell forward as she rested her face in the crook of her elbow.

Taking her hands, he stretched out her arms, guiding them to the front two legs of the ottoman. Now she was completely at his mercy, vulnerable…delectable. "How do you feel?" he asked softly, caressing the curves of her butt.

"Naughty."

The prompt one-word answer surprised a hoarse laugh from his oxygen-starved lungs. Any second now he would hyperventilate. "I'm okay with that," he said, grinning. "Since I'm about to ravish my lady lawyer."

She wriggled beneath his touch, her voice muffled. "I don't really think I'm your lawyer. In addition to my being on vacation, *this* would be a definite conflict of interest."

He leaned forward to kiss the back of her neck, brushing the hair aside. "Then perhaps you're my girlfriend. How does that sound?"

Beneath him, she went perfectly still. "Girlfriend?"

He rubbed his shaft in the cleft of her butt. "We're having sex. I'm wearing a tux tonight. Sounds like a relationship to me." And damned if he didn't like the idea. A lot.

"I'll take it under advisement."

Her wry comment would have bothered him had he not been so intent on hurrying things along. "Fair enough."

When he touched her between the legs, he found her damp and warm and ready. Brushing his fingertips over the place that made her groan with pleasure, he felt her tension rise.

"Pierce?"

He rested his whole weight on her for a moment, pressing

her into the cushion. "Hmm?" He grasped her wrists and manacled them to the wooden legs of the stool.

"Is this how you always have sex?"

"I can safely say it's a first for me."

"I can't decide if that makes me feel better or worse. Seems like *one* of us should have some experience."

"Don't worry, my sweet. I won't let you fall off."

"Such a gentleman."

Her low laugh raked across his nerve endings. His shaft hardened a millimeter more. He had reached the end of his patience. If he had his way, he would play with her all day and all night. But since he had come up short in the protection department, he'd have to make do with one intense coupling. And sometime before the gala, he was definitely going to hit up the drugstore for more condoms.

He reared back and took one last look at the beauty of her delicately etched spine. There, where her waist nipped in and her bottom flared, was a spot just made for a man's grasp. He rested one hand to steady himself and with the other guided his erection to the opening of her sex. Not bothering to remove her underwear, he shoved the minimal band aside.

Nudging the head of his shaft at her swollen flesh, he pushed inward. The color and light in her room didn't matter, because his eyes squeezed shut as he found his way to heaven. This angle was so much more stimulating. Or perhaps it was the caveman position...or the sound of Nikki's panting...or maybe even the way she lifted into his thrusts, as though fearing he might stop short.

She was tight. And hot. She had turned her head to one side, so he could see her profile. The small, straight nose, the softly curved lips, the eyelashes that rested in a crescent on her rosy cheek.

The rhythm of push and retreat made his scalp tingle

with the premonition of what was to come. He welcomed
the oblivion, courted it. Nikki squeezed him with hidden
muscles, shoving him closer to the edge. With both hands
on her bottom, he slammed into her, flesh to flesh, groan
to groan, hunger to hunger.

Sweat made his eyes sting. Or maybe it was the thought
of never having met her. Everything about her made him
crazy with wanting. Suddenly he felt the butterfly flutters
of her passage as she whimpered and arched her back in
climax. The extra dollop of stimulation snapped his control,
and he came hard, testing the limits of the little ottoman.

After that, things became hazy as he slumped on top of
her, trying to spare her his full weight. But his legs were em-
barrassingly weak, and his chest burned as he gasped for air.

"Sweet Lord." She had turned him inside out.

Nikki was quiet, too quiet. In sudden alarm, he rolled
to the floor and lay on his back so he could see her face.
Her eyes were closed, a tiny smile tilting the corners of
her mouth.

She was limp and sated, her body completely relaxed
on its perch. He tickled the side of her breast. "You still
breathing?"

Her tongue came out to wet her lips. "Barely." The word
was slurred.

"I don't suppose you have any idea what time it is?"

"Clock on the bedside table," she muttered.

He craned his neck. "Damn, damn, damn."

The one eyebrow he could see lifted. "Problem?"

"If I'm going to take you out on the town, we've got to
get a move on."

"I'll just stay right here," she said, the words drowsy.
"You can come back later."

"No way." He lurched to his feet and disposed of the condom. With one last look at the erotic picture she made, he

sighed and dragged her to her feet. "Hit the shower, woman. I'll pick you up in an hour and a half."

Nikki lifted her arms above her head and stretched. "If you say so."

He grabbed her up in a bear hug and pressed a kiss to her soft lips. "Don't be late. Or I might have to spank you."

"Promises, promises."

He made himself walk toward the door. But the last thing he saw as he looked wistfully over his shoulder was the sight of Nikki stepping out of her panties and sauntering toward the bathroom.

Nikki sat at one of many linen-clad tables for eight, the only person in residence at the moment on her particular island. The centerpieces across the room were elaborate arrangements of summer roses in cream, pink and soft yellow. Crystal sparkled. Silver gleamed. A stringed quartet played quietly in a far corner. Everything about the evening was a classy homage to wealth and privilege.

It takes money to make money. The old adage was true. Nikki had done enough charity work to know that these things followed a certain pattern. Court donors, thank donors, keep donors interested in the cause. Pierce was mingling, his stature and good looks making him hard to miss, even in the crowd. They were ensconced in the dining room of a stately old home in Charlottesville's historic district. Dinner had been lavish and delicious. Quail, summer vegetables, spinach soufflé, yeast rolls.

At the moment Nikki was finishing up her last bite of raspberry ice, which had been served with mint wafers and assorted dessert coffees.

Dancing would commence shortly in the grand ballroom, but at the moment, her tablemates, all of them board members and their spouses, were hobnobbing with VIPs. Since

Nikki knew virtually no one in the room, she had chosen to sit back and watch. Already both of Virginia's senators had made brief remarks before rushing off to the next item on their agendas.

Pierce joined her at last, reaching for his glass of ice water. "Well, I've done my part. Now we can have fun."

"What about the award?"

"We're waiting for the governor. Whenever he arrives, the dance floor will be cleared and we'll spend twenty or thirty minutes on the items listed in the program."

He stroked his hand down her arm. To the casual observer, the gesture would appear entirely proper. But Nikki shivered at the heat in his gaze. Deep, dark eyes gleamed with intent.

She sipped from her own water glass, flustered by the wash of heat at her throat. Pierce looked magnificent tonight. Chiseled jaw. Tanned skin above a snow-white shirt collar. His tux had clearly not been purchased off the rack. If fit him perfectly, revealing the width of his shoulders and the ripple of muscles in his powerful thighs and broad chest.

When she refused to meet his eyes, he leaned into her, their heads almost touching. "I can't wait to hold you in my arms," he said. His breath was warm on her cheek.

Such a simple statement. Yet so much unspoken.

At that moment, several members of their immediate party returned, forcing Pierce to remove himself to a respectable distance. As the others took their seats, laughing and talking and enjoying refills of wine, she wondered if any of them knew or cared that Pierce made her tremble just by sitting near her.

She dabbed her lips with a napkin. "Did you speak with your mother this afternoon?"

Pierce flinched. His gaze narrowed. "I called and told her I was back in town."

"And?"

"And that I had nothing to report."

His jaw jutted as though daring her to argue with him. But this was neither the time nor the place. "How's your dad?"

"Better. They're sending him home tomorrow. He'll still be receiving dialysis, of course, but as an outpatient."

"I'm glad he's improving."

"It's only a holding pattern. Without a kidney, he won't make it." She saw his hand grip a knife at his plate before he deliberately released it and swallowed half a glass of chardonnay in one gulp.

"Some people survive with one."

"If that one kidney is healthy. Dad has twenty percent function in one and fifteen in the other."

"I see." The prospect was indeed bleak. And she understood Pierce's desire to spare his mother pain. But his mom must surely be tormented with questions about her son's parentage. How could anyone put that aside? The uncertainty likely ate away at her. Nikki should know. She had firsthand knowledge about what kind of pain that futile wondering engendered.

A flurry of movement and noise signaled the moment to shift to the salon. Pierce took her hand and lifted her to her feet. His fingertips at her back, he ushered her ahead of him amid the press of guests walking and talking excitedly. This particular home had never before been opened to the public, so anticipation was high.

The magnificent room did not disappoint. Gleaming hardwood floors underfoot gave the feel of an earlier time. Enormous mirrors patterned after the hall at Versailles reflected colorfully dressed women and the black-and-white perfection of their escorts.

A small orchestra struck up the opening bars of a romantic Gershwin classic. Pierce smiled down at her. "I believe this dance is mine."

Her lack of experience was fortunately mitigated by her escort's athletic grace. He moved her across the floor with dexterity, pausing now and again to talk to friends and to introduce Nikki.

She felt like Cinderella at the ball. Certainly her background had not prepared her for this. Though she had learned to project confidence in most situations, even the most jaded of women might be swept off her feet in this fairy-tale setting.

Pierce's hand was warm on her back. They moved as one, perfectly in accord. Too bad they were not similarly aligned in their opinions about Pierce's past. She rested her head on his shoulder as the musicians lapsed into an even dreamier tune. If she could distill this moment and save it, she would. He was ruining her for other men.

She had done her research on the subject of the Wolff family this afternoon when Pierce was home getting ready. The press had plenty to say about the secretive billionaires. Reclusive…tightly knit…marked by tragedy. The patriarchs, brothers Victor and Vincent Wolff, were now old men. In the late seventies they had both married women fifteen years their junior. But in the 1980s Laura and Delores Wolff were kidnapped, held for ransom and later killed. Pierce would have been about five at the time if Nikki's math was right.

At that point the two grieving widowers, terrified for the safety of their children, had built an enormous house deep in the Blue Ridge Mountains. The home was referred to by locals and the press as Wolff Castle. The pictures Nikki had seen were impressive.

Both of the Wolff brothers had multiple children, Victor, three sons, and Vincent, one daughter and two sons.

And a third son he thought was dead.

A son who had no interest in embracing his roots, or so he said.

The dance drew to a close, and at a podium near one of the windows, a man stepped up to the mike and called for attention. Moments later the governor's entourage streamed into the room.

Pierce brushed her cheek with the back of his hand. "I've got to work my way to the front for my presentation."

"I never asked. Who's getting an award?"

"A local businessman who has been instrumental in organizing volunteers to maintain large sections of the trail not too far from here. He also gave a significant amount of money, but the award is for his grassroots activism. I won't be long."

Nikki stood, mostly unnoticed, near the navy velvet drapes flanking a window. Had she been so inclined, she could have perched quietly in the window embrasure. But she wanted to monitor the action.

The governor was charismatic, well spoken and suitably complimentary both of the area's natural beauty and of the conservancy's efforts to preserve the trail as a conduit for the nation's hikers. There was some political slant, but mostly a genuine appreciation of the group's purpose and efforts. When he was done, there were a few photo ops, and then it was time for the remainder of the program.

Nikki's heart beat with pride when Pierce took center stage to present his award. Articulate and sophisticated, he was equally at home in this rarefied social setting as he was climbing mountains and traversing rivers.

She glanced at the program she held and noticed that right at the end, there was to be a special guest. Pierce was momentarily trapped, since all of the board and the staff members were standing up front.

The conservancy's president made remarks next, and

then introduced his mystery guest, who stepped forward out
of the crowd. The president shook hands with the man and
spoke once more into the mike. "As many of you know, a series of severe storms has decimated portions of the trail. Although volunteer efforts are critical and much appreciated,
some of the repair work requires an influx of cash. Tonight
I am happy to introduce the man whose family has donated
five hundred thousand dollars for trail repair. Ladies and
gentleman, please help me welcome Mr. Devlyn Wolff."

Nikki's legs turned to jelly as a she heard the name roll
and echo in her head. Her gaze shot to Pierce, but he was not
looking at her. His face was blank, wiped clean of all expression. She was probably the only one in the room who had
any inkling that he had just been dealt an unexpected blow.

A man with Pierce's smile lifted a hand in response to
the crowd's roar of approval. Devlyn stood before the mi-
crophone, waiting until the noise died. "On behalf of my
entire family," he said, "it is my pleasure to make this do-
nation to the Appalachian Trail Conservancy. We value the
trail as a whole, but we have a special place in our hearts
for the portion that passes very near my family's home on
Wolff Mountain.

"The AT symbolizes all that is best about our country.
For a man or a woman to set foot on that long, winding path
stretching from Maine to Georgia means to disconnect from
the frantic pace of the twenty-first century and to reconnect
with our roots. We need the solace of wilderness to bring us
down to earth…literally. And to remind us that no matter
how far we progress in the realm of technology and communication, our most basic need is to recognize our humanity
and our bond with the natural world. I commend the many
volunteers who give so passionately of their time and talents.
And I hope that as each of you has the opportunity to be
out on the trail this year and in the years to come, either as

casual hikers or section hikers or the die-hard thru-hikers, you will take a moment to stop and listen to the wind as it speaks fleetingly of all who have gone before you.

"Thank you for your hospitality tonight, and thank you for protecting this beautiful place we call home."

Nikki blinked, and he was gone, swallowed up in a crowd of well-wishers. She was stunned. Breathless. Now that she knew the truth, there was no mistaking the resemblance between Devlyn Wolff and Pierce Avery. Though fraternal twins and not identical, there was symmetry in the way they held themselves and the way they spoke so passionately of nature and its influence on the quality of life.

Their coloring was similar. Warm golden skin, dark hair—though Devlyn's was more black than dark brown—and physical builds that were strong and powerful. Pierce had been standing only feet away from his blood brother. How could he turn his back on his family now?

She watched as the formalities ended and the dancing resumed. When Pierce rejoined her, she was shaking, her skin chilled and her head throbbing. It was so unfair. She had searched for years and with every means at her disposal to locate her parents. But to no avail. Yet Pierce, who already had a mom and dad who loved him, now found himself related to a family as fascinating and multilayered as the Kennedys.

He looped an arm around her shoulders. "You want to dance some more, or do we duck out of here?"

"Are you serious?" Her voice, uncomfortably high-pitched, skated up an octave or two.

"What's the problem, Nikki?" He sounded bored, as if he couldn't imagine why she was so upset.

She poked a finger in his chest. "That was your brother, damn it. Are you just going to let him walk away?"

Fourteen

Pierce was encased in a bubble of ice. Nothing could touch him. The surreal moment when he came face-to-face with a man eerily like himself was something he couldn't talk about. Somewhere beneath the chill was pain. A pain he couldn't handle right now. Maybe never.

Nikki's face was pale, her big eyes accusing him of God knew what. Why couldn't she simply enjoy the evening? He planned to.

She was dynamite in that sexy dress. It clung to every hill and valley of her body in a way that made him wish they were already alone. With her pale-blond hair and her regal posture, she put most of the women in the room to shame.

He removed her accusatory finger by kissing her hand. "Let's dance," he said, nuzzling her neck. Her light perfume and slender body rekindled his need to have her. How could he sate himself so recently and yet already want more?

Nikki trembled in his embrace, but this time it was not passion that made her shake. She took his hand and pulled him out of the room into an adjoining hallway. Allowing himself to be propelled by her urgency, he sighed when she found an empty room and dragged him inside.

He shut the door and leaned back against it, his arms crossed over his chest. "You surprise me, my lady lawyer. I didn't peg you as the type for indulging in a quickie at someone else's house."

"Don't," she said, her voice cracking. "Don't act like nothing has happened. Devlyn Wolff is your brother. I looked up the family this afternoon. Your aunt gave us your parents' names, so it wasn't hard to find information. You have another brother, as well, Larkin, and a sister, Annalise."

The words pierced his heart. Each one an inestimable pain. He didn't want to know these things…didn't want to think about what he had missed. *Siblings.* All his life he had longed for siblings.

He shrugged. "Everyone knows about the Wolffs. The paparazzi love them. But since I don't read the gossip rags, I could care less. I've had enough, Nikki. You're wasting your breath."

"We could probably catch him," she said, her gaze beseeching. "He only left moments ago, and the valet has to retrieve his vehicle. Let's go stop him. I'll explain. Tell him that we need to speak to his father."

"No, Nikki." He kept his expression impassive, his tone firm.

"But why?" Bewilderment filled her eyes.

"It's unnecessary. I don't plan to contact the Wolffs at all. So forget it. Just because you want to find out every last detail about your relatives doesn't mean I do. The status quo suits me very well. I don't need anything else."

"You're making a huge mistake," she cried.

Her passionate conviction gave him pause. But he couldn't afford to let doubt creep in. The consequences were too terrible to consider. What was he supposed to do? Go hat in hand, begging for a chance to graft himself onto the Wolff family tree? *Hell, no.*

"Maybe I am," he said. "But it's my mistake to make." He paused. "Here's the thing, Nikki." He took her hands in his, noting the icy skin and the tremor that spoke to her level of distress. Looking deep into her eyes, he spoke softly but distinctly. "I care about you a great deal. Perhaps more than you're willing to believe at this moment. I want to spend time with you. I want you in my bed…in my house. I want to show you my life and what I love and what I see for my future, perhaps our future. But…"

"But what?" She broke his gentle hold and backed away, her arms wrapped around her waist. The stance was self-protective. For the first time ever, he saw her as vulnerable. Nikki was always so strong, so confident, so full steam ahead. But now she seemed infinitely fragile, as though one wrong word from him could destroy her.

"If you want to be with me, you have to let this go."

She went white. "An ultimatum?"

"If you choose to call it that. All I'm asking is that you respect a personal boundary of mine. I would do the same for you."

"And that's it? We'll never speak of it again?"

He nodded. "That's what I want. That's the way it has to be."

He saw the muscles in her slender white throat work as she swallowed. "I don't know if I can…drop this incredible thing that we both know, I mean."

"Sure you can. Just imagine that we never went to see my aunt. That I never came to your office asking for help. That you and I met on a blind date and hit it off. Something like that."

Her eyes were dark and unreadable. "Those are a lot of lies to spin."

"Not lies." He winced, having founded his whole life

on integrity. "More like pleasant fiction. We aren't hurting anyone."

"Be honest with yourself, Pierce. You know it's not really true. To do what you're asking is hurtful both to your parents who raised you and to the man who thinks his son is dead."

"What they don't know *can't* hurt them."

"That's the kind of garbage rebellious teens tell themselves to justify lying to their parents and sneaking around doing things they shouldn't."

"So we're at an impasse. Is that what you're saying?" Nausea churned in his gut. He hadn't expected her to fight him on this. But he had clearly underestimated how much her past history affected her outlook.

For a moment, he pondered her reality: having no roots at all, no point of origin other than a home for children whose families either didn't exist or didn't want them. An icy sliver of shame snaked down his spine. What must Nikki think of him?

But even the jolt of genuine empathy he experienced for her heartbreakingly barren childhood couldn't sway him.

Nikki bowed her head, a swing of pale-blond hair obscuring her face momentarily. Despite this moment of emotional trauma, she was stunning. He wanted to go to her and take her in his arms and recreate the madness of the night before. But he sensed he had hurt her...had unwittingly struck at things so deeply ingrained in the fabric of who she was that her soul bled.

He could barely find his voice. "I asked you a question," he muttered. "Is this the end for us?"

She lifted her head slowly, her hands now clenched together, white-knuckled. "I need some time to think. Please take me home." The bleak acceptance in her gaze was another sin he had to bear.

"Of course. If that's what you want."

They made their way to the front of the house, not touching, not speaking. The car ride home was fraught with tension. At the curb in front of her building, he rested his hands on the steering wheel. "I'll come up and make sure you get in safely."

"No. I'd rather you didn't."

When she climbed out of the car, he followed suit, standing on the sidewalk with his hands in his pockets. He wanted her badly, but an agonizing chill iced his veins as he realized she was slipping away both physically and emotionally.

"A good-night kiss?" He tried to make the suggestion lighthearted.

Nikki pulled her pale, thin shawl closer despite the humid evening. "Please don't. Don't make this harder."

Anger won out, driven by desperation. "You're the one doing that."

She stumbled backward, a hand to her mouth. "I have to go."

As he watched, incredulous, she fled from him, easing through the front door and slamming it behind her.

It was at least five minutes before he turned to his car. Five long minutes when he wondered if he had made the biggest mistake of his life. But if having Nikki meant destroying his family and appealing to a clan legendary for their insularity, then he really had no choice.

Turning the key in the ignition, he forced himself to drive away without looking back.

Nikki was cold, so cold. Despite a blistering-hot shower and the comfort of a pair of fleecy winter pajamas, she couldn't stop shivering. The evening that had begun with such promise had ended in ashes.

Was Pierce right? Was it her fault they were not sharing a bed tonight? The evening of romantic music, intimate dancing, food, laughter and flirtation. All of it for naught, because she had seen Pierce's blood brother and that door, once opened, couldn't be closed. At least not in her mind.

She curled up on the sofa with an afghan, unable to stay more than a moment in her bedroom. The very air in there was so laden with memories of Pierce that she could not bear it. His wickedly sexy smile, his inventive love play, his fierce possession, his tender, arousing touch. The most wonderful moment of her life had gradually segued into another experience of loss.

And this time, at her own hand.

As the night waned, she stared blindly at the TV, the sound muted. Pierce had said he cared about her. He'd hinted at a future. But she was unable to get past this formidable stumbling block in the road. Pierce had discovered an incredible piece of news. He was a Wolff, a blood member of one of the country's most wealthy and influential and fascinating clans.

Why couldn't he acknowledge the import of what had happened?

She dozed occasionally, waking up time and again to the sick knowledge that nothing had changed. She was here... without him.

For a time, she felt so ill she wondered if she had caught something at the crowded party. Her limbs were weak and her stomach was unable to tolerate anything but ginger ale.

Toward morning, she fell into a light doze. The sun glaring in from a crack in the drapes finally woke her. She forced herself to get up, to move around the condo. Her lease was due for renewal in another three or four weeks. She had to decide whether to stay or go.

She liked her cozy home. It was a nest she had created from scratch, and she was proud of it. Though as a rule she was content with her quiet solitude, she did entertain from time to time, enjoying the company of friends she had made in Charlottesville, many of them young professionals like herself.

In the spare bedroom that passed for her home office, she picked up a folder containing the letter from her former law professor. She read it again, slowly, trying to decipher her own reactions. On the basis of this one piece of mail, she had decided to close her practice, even though deep in her heart she knew she didn't have any real desire to dissect the law at a big firm in D.C.

Her professor spoke highly of her work ethic, of her academic success and of his admiration for the sound start she had made with her practice in Charlottesville. He said he wanted her to join his team. That with her talent and drive she would have a shot at partner some day.

He said he wanted her.

That was it…the magic words that spoke of belonging and family. A work family, but a tie nevertheless. On the basis of that, Nikki had been ready to chuck everything she had begun in Virginia to head north, hoping to grab the brass ring on the merry-go-round.

She sank into a chair at the kitchen table, burying her face in her arms. What a liar she was. She'd told Pierce that she had put her past behind her, but she hadn't, not really. Otherwise, she could have been content with the way things were in her life, her *good* life. If she had truly made peace with the knowledge that her origins were a mystery, she wouldn't have reacted so strongly to Pierce and the shocking revelations that had rocked his world.

Sitting up, she saw the open box on the far counter. Several days ago, she had begun wrapping and packing some of her prized possessions. No china from a grandmother or crystal from a beloved great-aunt, merely department-store items with which she had set up housekeeping when she finished law school.

She knew her *things* were only things. That was a lesson she had learned early on. No matter how many trinkets a person bought, inanimate objects would never replace the love and affection of a family, of belonging. The little pewter collie she had rescued from her desk served to remind her of that.

So why was she about to throw the dice and bet on a future in D.C. when she had a man who cared about her here in Charlottesville?

The day passed slowly. Without question or doubt, she recognized that her future hung in the balance. She was a hundred percent sure she knew what she had to do, but she waited a couple more hours before picking up the phone and dialing the 202 area code.

The conversation was brief but cordial on both sides. When she hung up, she was pretty sure she smelled the acrid aroma of burning bridges.

But deciding what *not* to do was the easy part. Now the path ahead was murkier than ever.

She made herself a grilled cheese for supper, the first solid food she had eaten all day. Then she showered and changed into a sundress. Though she hadn't yet ventured outside, the TV weatherman claimed the city was about to break a record for summer heat.

Finally, she packed a small bag. The wise thing to do would be to call Pierce and see if he was home…to ask if he wanted to see her. But her emotions were too close to the surface. If she heard his voice, she might burst into tears. She wanted this reunion to be a happy one. And she had to get herself under control if that was to happen.

It was after seven when she gathered her purse and her bag and her keys. Locking the door behind her, she made her way downstairs. Her car was hot, so she lowered the windows and let the heavy summer air warm her skin. Gradually, as she drove out of town, a fragile sense of peace settled over her.

No decisions had been made. No momentous thresholds crossed. But for the moment it was enough that she wanted to be with Pierce.

As she drove through the trees lining his drive, she wondered if he would see her coming. Once she parked, she could hear the hounds baying behind the house. Evidently they served as visitor alarms.

Pierce emerged from the house as she got out of the car. He came down the steps immediately, whistling long and low. "Nice dress, lady lawyer. But not your usual style."

She shrugged. "It's hot."

"So it is."

Scintillating conversation. Taking a deep breath, she clenched her sweaty hands on the handle of her bag, keeping it between them for protection. Otherwise she might throw herself at him without a lick of modesty. "I have something important to tell you," she said.

His face changed. "Not now, Nikki. I don't want to argue tonight. I missed you like hell." He took the suitcase from her and set it on the bottom step. "Come here and kiss me."

Fifteen

Pierce was light-headed with relief. He hadn't meant to throw down a gauntlet yesterday, but Nikki's obsession with his Wolff connection was not something with which he could pretend to be okay. Leaving her last night had about killed him. So much so that for a moment or two today, he had actually contemplated getting in touch with Vincent Wolff.

Even the thought of it made him violently ill. Every cell in his body screamed out in repudiation when he imagined what such a contact would do to his beloved parents. Even for Nikki, he simply couldn't do it.

Thank God she had come to him.

His arms settled around her waist as she laid her head on his chest. He felt her sigh.

"I missed you, too," she said.

Whatever she wanted to say to him could wait until morning. He had plans for tonight.

She was wearing a thin cotton sundress with a skirt that fluffed out from a tiny waist. The pale mint-green fabric trimmed in white lace left her shoulders bare and made her look young and carefree. But the dark circles beneath her eyes, the smudges she had tried to disguise with makeup, told another story.

He lifted her chin with his thumb and lowered his mouth to hers. "Thank you for coming back to me." He tasted her, feasted on her. Her kiss was open and generous, and he felt like a cad for hurting her. Long and slow, the kiss ran its course. They were standing outside, but there were no witnesses this time, no one to interrupt, save the dogs baying mournfully out back.

He cupped the back of her neck with his hand, feeling the delicate skin at the top of her spine. Her hair spilled like gold silk over his fingers. Lust roared hot and thick through his veins, fueled by the recognition of how near he had come to losing her.

Pulling her even closer, he pressed his hips to hers, frustrated by the layers of cloth between them. If they went inside the house, he'd be on her like a madman. In fact, he was perilously close to sitting on the step and letting her straddle his lap. But he owed her more than this. She'd had the courage to come back. So he would give her the wooing she deserved.

Clearing his throat, he released her, feeling the loss in every bone and muscle. "I have an idea," he said, the words gravelly.

She smiled at him, a small smile, but a smile nevertheless. "Yes?"

"Do you like horses?"

The smile dimmed. "I have no real frame of reference. But I guess they're okay."

"It's a beautiful night," he cajoled. "Why don't you let me take you for a ride? I'll have my arms around you. You'll be perfectly safe."

Glancing down at her dress, she wrinkled her nose. "I didn't bring a riding wardrobe."

"Not a problem. I like you in that dress. Makes me thing of the sherbet my grandma used to give me on summer days like this one." Nostalgia turned to sadness as he realized that even his extended family wasn't his to claim anymore. He took her hand. "Come on. You'll love it, I promise."

It didn't take a genius to sense her ambivalence, but after he grabbed her things and put them inside, she followed him around the house anyway. At the stable he perched her on a bale of hay while he saddled a docile mount. The old palomino was one he'd ridden as a boy. Her most onerous task these days was swishing flies with her tail. But though she was not technically useful as a work animal, or even for serious riding, Pierce would let her live out her days in peace.

When the saddle and tack were positioned to his liking, he walked her out of the stall to where Nikki sat, legs crossed pretzel-style like a little girl, her hands on her knees.

Her eyes widened. "It's awfully big."

"She's a *she,* and I first rode her when I was five years old. The old girl is as docile as a clump of daisies. In fact, that's her name…Daisy."

He tied the horse to a fence post and then coaxed Nikki to her feet. "Don't be afraid. Daisy is a sweetheart. Leave your sandals here. They'll only fall off along the way, and I don't want to lose them."

When she stood barefoot, looking up at him with barely veiled apprehension, he wanted nothing more than to spread that fresh, clean hay, grab a blanket and take her beneath the sun-streaked skies. Instead, he lifted her by the waist and seated her at the front of the large saddle.

"What do I do?" she gasped, her cheeks flushed with color.

"Hold on to the pommel horn." In the process of straightening Nikki's skirts, he inadvertently touched one of her firm, pale thighs. Stifling a groan of sexual frustration, he made sure she was decently covered before putting a foot in the stirrup and swinging up behind her.

He took the reins in his right hand and curled his left arm around her waist, pulling her firmly into the notch of his thighs. His sex was rigid and full, but he doubted Nikki noticed. She was breathing so fast, hyperventilation was a real possibility.

"Relax, honey." He kissed the side of her neck. "I won't let you fall, I swear." Deciding that nothing would convince her but actual experience, he urged Daisy into a slow trot.

Nikki's spine was straight, her eyes focused straight ahead. "I don't think I'm ready for this."

"Too late."

He grinned, loving the moment when that prissy spine lost its starch and Nikki relaxed against his chest. He picked up speed, not enough to alarm his passenger, but enough to make the breeze sweep over them in cooling waves. Little by little he showed her the expanse of his property.

Finally he heard her laugh. And that was when he knew he had made a convert. "You want to try a flat-out gallop?"

Her head whipped around so fast he tasted a mouthful of hair. "No. I mean it, Pierce. I don't want to."

"All right, Ms. Chicken. We'll work up to that." He took the opportunity to kiss her. Nikki's sigh of surrender melted into the faint sounds of summer…tree frogs, faraway lawn mowers, the twitter of birdsong as the shadows elongated.

He moved his mouth over hers roughly, letting her feel the full extent of his hunger. She was eager and responsive in return. For a split second he considered the logistics of sex on horseback. He'd read that it was possible, but with a perfectly good king-sized bed at his house, it seemed less than prudent to try.

He ran his thumb along her jawline. "Ready to go back?" They were barely a mile from home.

Arousal darkened her eyes and colored her cheekbones. "Yes. If you are."

He turned Daisy in an easy circle. "I was ready the minute you got out of the car. But I was trying to be a gentleman."

When she laughed softly, the hair stood up on his arms. He was wound so tightly, even the sound of her voice was almost enough to tip him over.

As they cantered back down the trail, Nikki hummed snatches of tunes he didn't recognize. Probably because the wind caught them and carried them away. She was no longer clutching the saddle. Instead, she nestled in his embrace as if they had been doing this for years.

At the door to the barn, he pulled up short and jumped down from the saddle. Nikki held out her arms and leaned toward him. He lifted her off the horse with care. Deliberately, he let her slide down the length of his body, very slowly. Now there was no way she could miss his erection. It pulsed and throbbed between them with an insistence that would no longer be denied.

"Give me five minutes," he said, kissing the top of her head.

In the barn, poor Daisy received only the most cursory of care. He removed the saddle, made sure she had oats and water and locked her in for the night.

Nikki, when he spotted her, was leaning against the corral rail, the skirts of her dress whipping in the wind. A thunderstorm, sparked by the stifling heat, brewed in the distance.

"We'd better get inside," he said. "Those clouds look nasty."

Nikki turned and leaned back on the fence, her expression odd.

"What's wrong?" he asked, studying her face with some alarm.

"I never knew riding a horse was so...well..." She grimaced.

As she shifted from one foot to the other, he suddenly understood. "Is my lady lawyer a little chafed?" He lifted her skirt and lightly touched the inside of her thigh. "Right here?"

Nikki bit her lip and nodded.

Pierce dropped to his knees, gathering the cloth of her dress in his hands. Sure enough, a red line on either leg marked the places where the saddle had rubbed her uncomfortably. He kissed each spot tenderly. "I'm sorry, my love. I never should have made you go in that dress. But I have to admit I liked it. Knowing that you were wearing nothing but those tiny panties."

From the expression on her face, he could see that they were both thinking of their footstool escapade.

She licked her lips. "It's fine. I have some lotion in my bag."

The words were prosaic, but they made his fever worse. A crack of thunder in the distance galvanized him. "Come on."

Just as they reached the porch, fat drops of rain began pelting down. Larry, Moe and Curly had taken refuge in their sturdy doghouse. As Pierce and Nikki watched, jagged streaks of lightning lit up the sky. One strike that was a bit too close for comfort sent them scrambling inside.

Pierce scooped Nikki into his arms and started up the stairs.

She looped one arm around his neck and grinned. "Aren't you going to feed me a late dinner?"

He paused, three steps from the top. "Seriously?"

"No. I ate a long time ago. Carry on."

"Thank God."

His fervent response made her laugh again. He hadn't paused to pick up her luggage, but that could wait for later. Right now he had plans that included Nikki being naked.

He reached the door to his bedroom, carried her over the threshold and moved toward the bathroom. When he set her on her feet, he saw her glance at the huge mirror that covered half of one wall. "Are you showering?" she asked, her gaze demure.

"*We're* showering," he said, stripping off his shirt, boots, pants and boxers.

Nikki's eyes widened.

"Too fast?" he asked, reaching into the shower to turn on the water.

Her gaze was fixed on his sex. "No. A shower would feel great."

She reached behind her for the zipper, but he turned her around. "Let me do that." Lowering the zip carefully, he uncovered, bit by bit, her narrow-waisted, pale-skinned back. A tiny mole high on her left shoulder blade begged for a kiss.

Nikki held the bodice of her dress to her chest. "Pierce?"

"Hmm?" He was busy running his hands over the curves of her butt.

"When we're done, I need to talk to you about something important. I did something I'm not sure you'll approve of."

He froze inwardly. *Damn it*. He had a good idea what she was going to say. And deep in his gut he knew that he would eventually have to acknowledge the fact that things had changed. But not now. Not with her in his bedroom. "It can wait until tomorrow, Nikki. Let me have this one night. Please."

His answer seemed to trouble her, but she nodded her head slowly. "All right. If that's what you want."

"I do." He pried her fingers from the edge of the fabric. The pretty little dress fell to the tile floor, leaving its owner clad in nothing but champagne silk panties.

He swallowed hard, his throat tight. Her breasts were full and high, the nipples dark pink. He rubbed the centers with his thumbs. "I can't imagine never having met you." Already she seemed a central part of his life. He was falling in love with her. And the thought didn't even scare him. If she wanted to take the D.C. offer, they would work something out. Somehow. But he wasn't going to let her go. That much was clear.

He tested the water with one hand and found it warm and ready. Drawing her into the walk-in shower enclosure, he laughed softly as the stream sluiced over them, washing away the stickiness from the heat and humidity. Grabbing a bar of soap, he ran it over Nikki's breasts, again and again.

"I'm clean," she gasped, her eyes half closed. She lifted her face to the water, rubbing both hands over her cheeks. "This feels so good."

Good indeed. He moved to other parts of her body, her feet, her legs, the tender flesh inside her upper thighs. Nikki's hands splayed on the shower wall, her head bent. "I hope you have a big hot water heater," she quipped. But despite her humor, she moaned when he moved to more intimate areas. This time, he took a washcloth and soaped it up. Carefully, he moved it over her sensitive sex.

The deliberate attention was giving Nikki pleasure. And there was pleasure for him in it as well. But his control was shot. With one last pass of his fingers, he stepped away and dragged in a much-needed gasp of air. "All done," he croaked.

Nikki looked over her shoulder, her eyelids drooping and her lips puffy from his earlier kisses. "You're very good at that," she complained. "But I don't really suppose I want

to know how many women you've entertained in this he-
donistic bathroom."

"You're the first," he said simply. "I like my privacy."

"But then I intruded today and you didn't have the heart
to tell me to leave."

He shook his head. "You intruded into my life, and I
liked it. Hence the shower invitation."

Her hands went to his shaft, gathering him into her soapy
hands. "You are a very beautiful man. I think I would like
to see you in action on the river some day. From a safe distance."

As she caressed him slowly, his knees locked and his
groin tightened. "I could teach you how to kayak…in calm
water."

"But it's not as much of a challenge that way, is it? And
you thrive on challenge." She ran her fingers from the base
of his erection to the crown with just the right pressure. "I
would never want to change who you are, Pierce. Everything
you love scares me to death, but it makes you who you are."

He was at the end of his patience. "You scare me," he
said, with absolute truth. He had no idea how to make her
happy, and yet she had come back to him of her own accord. Turning the faucet, he shut off the water. The sudden
silence was shocking.

He reached for two towels and handed her one. It was
not possible for him to dry her or to allow her to touch him
either. Only one thing was left to do. He waited impatiently
until her hair was only damp and her skin glowed rosy red
from a brisk rubdown. "Come to bed with me," he said. He
dragged her into the bedroom. "I can't wait another second."

Sixteen

Nikki was as eager as he was. This relationship might not last past the week, so she wanted as much time with him as possible. She crawled onto the mattress and scuttled beneath the covers. Her damp hair and the air conditioning combined to chill her skin, despite the pumping of blood in her veins.

Her limbs felt clumsy and uncoordinated. Her sex ached and pulsed with needs that overwhelmed her with their insistence. She had never considered herself a highly sexed person, but with Pierce she appeared to have a voracious appetite for sensual pleasure.

After rolling on a condom, he moved on top of her, supporting his weight on his arms. She wanted to tell him about her call to D.C., but he had put her off. Would he think that she had turned down the job because of him? That was partly true. But she didn't want him to think she was making assumptions about their future.

She was beginning to see that Pierce could be the man in her life…always. Though just because she was there emotionally didn't mean he was. Which was why she needed to tell him soon. And if he asked what she planned to do, she would have to be honest: she didn't know. But she was willing to stay in Charlottesville to find out.

Above them, powerful rain drummed a harsh rhythm on the roof. Lightning flashes illuminated the room in crazy intervals. He spread her legs with his thighs. "I don't want to fight with you," he said hoarsely, his eyes shadowed.

Yesterday he had told her without equivocation that if she wanted to be with him, she had to forget about the Wolffs. She would try. But she had to hope that he would eventually change his mind.

She touched his face, holding his cheeks with her hands. He hadn't shaved today, and the stubble was rough beneath her fingertips. "I don't want to fight, either. We both have pretty strong opinions. So we're bound to clash occasionally. But that doesn't have to be the core of our relationship. I'd rather make love, not war."

He nodded slowly. "I couldn't agree more." He moved his hips, his shaft pushing at her entrance. "Starting right now."

The joining of their bodies was as straightforward and easy as nature itself. But for Nikki, it was cataclysmic. The sense of homecoming, of connectedness, brought tears to her eyes.

Pierce brushed away one that escaped and rolled down her cheek. "Don't cry, Nikki. We'll make this work."

He was talking about her job offer, and she felt a stab of guilt for not including him in her decision. Not that they were an official couple. But he deserved to know that she had recognized her need to be wanted…to belong. Some men didn't like clingy women. Nikki portrayed to the world a far more confident persona than the scared little girl who always knew she wouldn't be picked. So she wasn't really being honest with him.

She curled her legs around his waist, loving the sensation of fullness, of heat and completion. "I'm not used to having someone to answer to," she said softly. "And I tend to be stubborn sometimes."

"I've noticed. But I'm not the world's most flexible guy either. Perfection is boring. And you sure as hell never bore me, Nicola Parrish."

"I'm pretty sure there was a slur in their somewhere." She laughed softly, and then gasped when he withdrew briefly only to thrust hard and deep in the next second.

He lowered his head to kiss her, sliding his tongue into her mouth and mimicking the action of his lower body. "You taste like a man's wildest dreams."

She returned the kiss lazily, curling her tongue around his and making him groan. When she nipped his bottom lip with her teeth, he cursed. Her hands roved the damp planes of his back, the muscular shoulders, the smooth, hot skin. His weight pressed her into the mattress, and she liked it. Rather than any feeling of being trapped, it was a delicious sensation of safety and sheer wonder.

Her interest in analyzing the situation was fast being replaced by an intense race to the finish. Pierce's eyes were closed, his face a mask of masculine determination as he moved in her forcefully.

Heat coiled low in Nikki's abdomen, her breath caught, and she cried out as a stunning climax snatched her up, tumbled her in waves and slowly eased her onto the opposite shore.

She held Pierce as he came, his big body shuddering, helpless, as he thrust into her again and again. At last, it was over.

In the silence that followed, she heard the rain diminish to a light patter. Moments after that, it stopped completely. In the far distance, soft rumbles marked the path of the storm as it moved away.

Pierce rolled to his side and gathered her close. "Stay with me tonight," he said, his body already lax.

She nodded sleepily. "I'm not going anywhere."

It was the most restful night of sleep Pierce had experienced since finding out he wasn't an Avery. He awoke only once, around 3:00 a.m., at which time he tiptoed downstairs to make sure everything was locked up tightly. In his rush to get Nikki into bed, he hadn't followed his usual nighttime routine.

Standing in his darkened kitchen drinking a glass of milk, he realized that he *needed* Nicola Parrish, maybe even *loved* her, though he wasn't quite willing to put a name to his muddled emotions just yet. Whatever his future held, he sensed that it included Nikki. He couldn't imagine not having her upstairs in his bed. Every night. All night. With her, his life made sense. Even amid the shambles of his discoveries about his paternity.

But he felt instinctively that it was too soon to tell her. They had to deal with the Wolff situation, even if that meant asking Nikki to keep the secret forever. Aunt Trudie was the only other person who knew, and she was so old and frail, her knowledge might die with her very soon.

And then there were Pierce's parents, his very ill father and his completely confused mother. What should Pierce do in those situations? Selfishly, he wanted to confess his love and bind Nikki to him, concentrating on nothing but making her happy. In an ideal world, that would be an acceptable choice. But for now he would keep his own counsel. She would not expect any kind of declaration this soon in their relationship. Pierce would have to be patient…and wait.

As he climbed back into bed, she stirred. "You okay?"

He smoothed a hand down her belly to the place where

she felt damp and swollen. "I can't get enough of you." It was the stark truth.

She sighed, a long exhalation of pleasure. "Then take what you want, Mr. Avery. I'm all yours...."

The next time he awoke, the sun was high in the sky, the morning well on its way. He dressed quietly and sneaked outside to feed the dogs and to check on the other animals. When that was done, he entered the house and listened. Still no movement in the bedroom up above.

He decided that brunch would be a good idea. As he scrambled eggs and fried bacon, a sound on the stairs caught his attention. Nikki stood on the third step to the bottom, a bashful smile on her face. "I didn't have my suitcase," she said.

Which explained why she was wearing the sundress again. If she was planning to get clean undies from her bag, then at the moment she was probably bare underneath. That one thought was all it took to make him hard all over again.

He cleared his throat. "Food's ready. You want to eat?"

She nodded. "I'm starving."

There was tension at the table. He couldn't decide if it was simply morning-after awkwardness or something more.

He finished his meal and put down his fork. "You were going to tell me something last night, and I wouldn't let you."

She blushed. "Well, I made a phone call..."

Just then, the doorbell rang. Grumbling inwardly, he pushed back his chair and went to answer it. The open floor plan of his house was one he had designed, but at moments like these, there was nowhere for Nikki to hide if she was embarrassed.

He flipped the lock and opened the door. A man stood there wearing a snappy three-piece suit, despite the heat.

He was older, perhaps even in his seventies. The briefcase he carried was well-worn.

Pierce kept the door only partially open. From past experience, he knew some salesmen were ballsy enough to stride right in if given half an inch. "May I help you?"

The man looked him over, curiosity in his gaze. "If you are Pierce Avery, I'd like to speak with you."

Pierce nodded. "I am. And who are you?"

"I'm an attorney representing Mr. Vincent Wolff."

Pierce flinched. "Not interested." He tried to close the door, but the man inserted a foot and pushed back.

"It's important that we talk, Mr. Avery."

Rage boiled up, bitter and black. "I have no connection to the Wolffs. You're wasting your time."

"Mr. Wolff received a phone call yesterday…"

Pierce fell back half a step, shock stealing his breath. He turned and found Nikki staring at him, anxiety all over her face. Please, God. She didn't. She couldn't have. Not when he had made his feelings so crystal clear…

Ruthlessly, he clamped down on his emotions. He would not give either of them the satisfaction of seeing him implode. Facing the intruder once more, he firmed his jaw. "Leave. Now. Or I'll have you arrested for trespassing."

The man had no choice but to depart. Before he left, however, he tossed his business card on a table just inside the foyer. "When you change your mind, please call me."

Pierce slammed the door and stood facing it as he counted to twenty as slowly as he could. He didn't trust himself not to do something violent.

Turning to face Nikki, he spoke calmly and without inflection. "Get out of my house."

She paled. "But Pierce—"

He cut her off with a slash of his hand. "Here's your bag. Take it and go. I don't want to see you again."

I made a phone call. Remembering her words made him sick.

Tears spilled down Nikki's cheeks. "Let me explain, Pierce. It's not what you think."

He flung the door wide open and threw her small piece of luggage down the stairs with all the force he could muster. It bounced and tumbled and landed against the back tire of her car. He told himself it was fury he felt. Not betrayal or grief, or loss. The pain in his chest spread to his limbs. "I have things to do, Ms. Parrish. Get out."

She walked toward him, her spine straight and her head held high. But on her face he saw the twin demons of fear and regret.

When she stepped past him out onto the porch, he inhaled the scent of her perfume. It clung to his sheets upstairs. He would burn them. That's all. And she'd be erased.

He forced himself to watch her depart. She tripped on the bottom step and fell to her hands and knees on the concrete drive. Clinging to the edge of the door, he refused to go to her aid. It was no more than she deserved. She picked herself up, ignored her bloodied extremities, and put her suitcase in the backseat.

Without once looking toward him or the house, she got in and drove away.

For an hour Pierce paced the floors of his big, lonely house. It had never seemed lonely before. Damn her. Just after two o'clock, the doorbell rang again. His heart leaped in his chest even as his jaw turned to granite. A woman who could be that duplicitous would get no shrift from him.

He answered the summons calmly, though inside he was a mess. "What now?"

But it wasn't Nikki. Nor was it the other lawyer. This time, a different man stood on the steps. He paled when he saw Pierce. And grabbed his chest. Alarmed, Pierce ushered him inside, moving him quickly to the sofa. The man stared…just stared.

Pierce brought him a glass of water. "Drink this."

The man complied. Gradually some of the color returned to his face. The entire time, his gaze tracked Pierce compulsively.

Pierce was at the end of his patience. "As I told the first lawyer, I have no connection to the Wolff family. You can go back and tell them I said so. Maybe he was the B team and now they've sent in the big guns, but my answer is still the same."

The man with the white hair and the large beak of a nose glared. "My name is Vincent Wolff. I think I am your father."

The room did a sudden kaleidoscope whirl. Pierce felt his heart beating in his ears. "I already *have* a father."

"And you have brothers and cousins and a sister and an uncle. I'm sending a helicopter for you at five o'clock. I want to introduce you to all of them."

Pierce felt the noose tightening around his neck. "This knowledge you think you have is supposition only."

Vincent snorted. "Now that I've seen you, I've got no doubts. You and Devlyn may not be identical, but the Wolff gene is strong in you."

Pierce thought of his mother and his father in a hospital room. That memory bolstered his resolve. "I don't really care what you think. The Wolffs are nothing to me."

Vincent got to his feet, his brow beaded with sweat. "What are you afraid of, boy?"

"I'm not afraid of anything."

But that was a lie. He was afraid his father was never going to get well. He was afraid his mother would look at him differently if she knew the truth. He was afraid that if he admitted he was a Wolff, his whole world would change.

Vincent must have read the turmoil in his face, because his fierce scowl softened. "We want to know you, Pierce. That's all. No expectations. No demands. We are not a threat."

Pierce swallowed. Despite his resistance, the truth was inescapable. This man who had come down from his mountaintop and sought him out was blood kin. That kind of connection transcended reason and operated on a visceral level.

"I appreciate your invitation, sir. But I'm not sure this is the time."

"We've waited over thirty years. I'd say that's long enough."

Pierce's phone rang, startling both of them. When he glanced at the number and saw that it was his mom, his heart thudded unpleasantly. "I need to take this."

Vincent nodded. "Of course." He wandered to the opposite side of the room.

Pierce answered the call. "Mom? What is it?"

She began talking rapidly, and Pierce sank into a chair, his legs weak. At long last, he got a word in edgewise. "Tell Dad I love him. And I love you, too. Talk to you later."

When he looked up from the phone, Vincent stared at him. "Your parents?" The words seemed to stick in the old man's throat.

Pierce nodded. "Yes. My dad…he…" Damn, this was awkward. "He's been waiting months for a kidney donor. That was my mother telling me they've finally found one. The surgery will be next week."

"Congratulations."

"Thank you."

"Will you come to Wolff Mountain?" The diffident request held no heat. Only a poignant supplication.

Relief about his father's good news enveloped Pierce. In

some weird way, the phone call had caused a shift in the room. On Vincent's face he saw the years of grief and the dawn of hope. Pierce's prayers had been answered. His father would live.

Perhaps it was time to pay it forward.

"Yes," Pierce said slowly. "I guess I will."

Nikki cried until her eyes were puffy and her cheeks were blotchy and red. She had never seen Pierce so angry, and it was partly her fault for handling things so poorly. The night of the gala he had asked her if she could leave the Wolff thing alone and she had told him she didn't know.

So when the lawyer showed up, Pierce had thought the worst.

What a mess.

At last she washed her face and tried to make a plan. If this was the end, she needed to quit painting rosy pictures of a future with Pierce. She was an independent woman who had spent most of her life alone. Even with a broken heart, she would force herself to pick up the pieces and start over.

Perhaps it might have made a difference if she had told Pierce she loved him. Perhaps then he would not have been so quick to think she had betrayed him. But in his shoes, wouldn't she have jumped to the same conclusions? No one else knew the secret but Gertrude. And it was almost impossible to believe that the old woman had finally broken her silence and gone to the Wolffs.

With a pad and pen in her hand, Nikki curled up on the sofa and began a list of objectives to get her life on track. Hovering just offstage was a debilitating pain because she had lost the one person who seemed to *want* her. In every way. But she had experienced loss before, and she knew better than most that no one really dies of a broken heart.

When her cell phone rang, she started to ignore it. Probably one of her ex-clients, having a hard time severing the cord. With a sigh, she reached into her purse and then froze when she read the number.

She picked up the phone. "Hello?"

"To be clear, I'm calling about your legal services." Her heart sank. Pierce's voice was familiar but cool. "I'm being summoned to Wolff Mountain for dinner. I'd like you to go with me."

"I don't think it's necessary for you to have representation in a casual setting. And considering the nature of our personal relationship, it's even less of a good idea."

"We have no personal relationship," he said curtly. "You owe me this. They're sending a helicopter at five. Be here or I'll come drag you out of that condo."

"Pierce, I…" She wanted to explain that she hadn't made the call to the Wolffs, but in his current mood, he was not going to listen. "I'll be there," she said, with a hitch in her words, her voice dull. Under no scenario could she imagine an evening any worse. But if Pierce wanted her in attendance, she would go.

Because, for better or worse, she loved him.

Seventeen

Pierce stood on his front porch and watched the black-and-yellow chopper land in the field. Nikki had arrived moments before but was still in her car. When she got out, his heart gave a funny kick. She looked nothing like the sleep-rumpled female in the wrinkled sundress who had appeared in his kitchen only that morning.

This woman was poised from head to toe, not a blond hair out of place. Her dress was black, some kind of knit fabric that clung to her as she walked. A modest V-neck and three-quarter-length sleeves made it an entirely suitable choice for dinner with a family of billionaires. She wore heels, black as well, but they were not outrageously high.

When she approached him, he had to fight to keep from reaching for her. She was beautiful and remote, her gaze barely acknowledging him before skittering away. *He* was the one responsible for the distance between them. "They're ready for us," he said.

Nikki nodded, her eyes fixed on the helicopter. Her shoes were not ideal for walking across a grassy meadow, but she managed without his help. He had a feeling she would have ignored his hand even if he had offered it.

Once airborne, it was too noisy for conversation. The pilot soared over the city, soon leaving civilization behind to head deep into the mountains. By car, the trip would have taken much longer. But as the crow flew, it lasted barely fifty minutes. The landing was smooth and uneventful.

A Jeep awaited them at the helipad. A young man in crisp khakis and a knit shirt with a Wolff Enterprises logo greeted them, tucked their luggage in the back of the Jeep and stood at attention, politely waiting for them to climb in.

Nikki looked at Pierce briefly. "I'll get in the back," she said.

He frowned. "Don't be ridiculous. Not in that dress." He folded himself up for the short stint, thus being forced to look at the back of Nikki's neck...her graceful, pale-skinned neck. It was impossible not to relive every moment he had kissed that exact spot. He shifted uneasily in his seat. "Are they expecting us this soon?"

The driver nodded. "Yes, sir. The whole family is in residence on the mountain, even Devlyn and Gillian, who live in Atlanta."

Pierce grew increasingly disturbed as the house came into view. Perched in a saddle between two outcroppings on the mountaintop, the term *house* was somewhat of a misnomer. The locals called it Wolff Castle. With its massive size and crenellated battlements, the structure made an impression. Pierce was fairly certain that was the intent.

When they pulled up in the circular flagstone driveway, a lone figure came out to greet them. Vincent Wolff.

He helped Nikki out of the vehicle and stared at her. "Are you his girlfriend?"

Nikki shook her head instantly. "No, sir, I'm his—"

Pierce stopped her with a hand on her arm. "She's my friend. I thought I might need reinforcements."

Vincent chuckled, but the sound was rusty, as though he seldom laughed. "Fair enough."

Pierce stood for a moment, soaking in the feel of the place. At this altitude, the light breeze seemed almost cool, despite the late-summer heat in the valley. He cocked his head, meeting Vincent's pointed stare with a rueful shrug. "I'm not quite sure how we go about this."

Vincent nodded. "Nor am I. The entire group, minus the children, of course, has convened in the dining room. I've told them you're my son, but not much else. I thought it would be easier to explain to everyone at once."

"They're not going to be happy about this."

Vincent frowned. "What do you mean?"

"I imagine they'll all be wondering how much their inheritance is going to dwindle. With another mouth to feed."

The Wolff patriarch was visibly irritated. "Don't be ridiculous. We have more money than we know what to do with, and I happen to know that you're a wealthy man in your own right."

"Not like this." Pierce's laconic reply was nothing less than the truth. It was hard to imagine what kind of fortune it had taken to build such an enormous dwelling in this remote location.

Though Pierce would happily have dawdled outdoors forever, putting off what was to come, Vincent ushered them inside. "We don't bite," he said, accurately reading Pierce's mood.

Nikki was a silent, watchful presence through it all. Though Pierce would never have admitted it—not with things the way they were—having her here comforted him in ways he couldn't explain.

Stepping across the threshold into the dining room was one of the hardest things he had ever done. Nikki laid her hand on his forearm and squeezed gently before releasing him. Her unspoken support was both helpful and hurtful. If it hadn't been for her, he wouldn't have to be here doing this thing he didn't want to do.

There were three empty seats at the table. Vincent indicated spots for his two guests and took the remaining chair. Thirteen pairs of eyes stared at them.

Pierce cleared his throat and lifted a hand. "Hello. I'm Pierce Avery. This is Nikki Parrish."

The dead silence remained heavy and ominous.

Pierce looked at Vincent and shrugged. "This is your show," he said, trying not to sound like a complete jackass. What on earth did the old man hope to accomplish?

Vincent stared at the group assembled around the table, his age-spotted hands trembling where they lay clasped in front of him.

Pierce took stock as well. The men were handsome and broad-shouldered and bore a strong resemblance to each other. The women were more varied in terms of hair color and build. Pierce knew that three of the men were Victor's sons and that two others and one of the women were Vincent's children. The only one he recognized was Devlyn, the Wolff who had presented a check at the gala.

Finally, Vincent spoke. "I've told all of you that this man is my son. And I suppose you think I had some long-ago affair. But the truth is so much more complicated."

Pierce kept his eyes on the old man, unable to deal with the curiosity on the faces of everyone who watched him. Nikki's chair was close to his, and though she wasn't touching him, he had a sense that she was somehow guarding him. The notion was foolish, but he could actually feel the heat from her body.

Victor spoke up. "Don't keep us in suspense any longer. Tell us the tale."

Vincent nodded. "I'll start at the beginning, then. You

may not know this, but when Delores and I started trying to have a family, there were problems. She had two miscarriages. When we finally found out she was pregnant, we were over the moon. Her personality was mercurial at times, so I worried a bit about the pregnancy, but if anything, it served as a mood booster. And each trimester was better than the last.

"When it came time to deliver, we headed for the hospital." He paused suddenly and looked at Pierce and Nikki. "Victor and I lived in Charlottesville back then…Wolff Mountain didn't come along until five years later…when both Laura and Delores were taken from us."

Pierce nodded tersely. After Nikki had admitted to researching the Wolffs, Pierce had done so as well. He'd read the tragic accounts of the kidnapping during a shopping trip. Despite a ransom being paid, the two young Wolff wives had been murdered in cold blood. He shivered as if a ghost had flitted through the room. Had things been different, he would have lost his mother at a young age.

Vincent continued, the cynosure of all eyes. "The labor was long…as is often the case with first babies, but Delores did well. I was in the delivery room part of the time, because she wanted me there. But I stepped out often. Men of my generation were not as involved as dads are now. It was the one time when I keenly felt the fifteen-year gap between my young wife and myself."

He smiled wryly. "Anyway, I had been in the hallway grabbing a cup of coffee when there was some kind of hubbub in the delivery room. Panicked, I went back in and saw that all the nurses and the doctor were laughing and even crying.…"

He took a deep breath. Everyone around the table seemed to lean forward.

"We had twins," he said simply. "It was a miracle. We

were on the cusp of the time before ultrasounds were commonplace, and our doctor did not use them. During the pregnancy, one baby had hidden, as they call it, behind the other, so the doctor had only ever heard one heartbeat.

"Delores was in shock, as was I, but oh, the joy…" He wiped his eyes and blew his nose on a handkerchief. Tucking it back in his pocket, he continued. "The babies were born in the wee hours, so no family was with us at that point. We decided to save our news for the morning. And since we were exhausted, we sent the babies to the nursery for a little while so we could get some rest."

His throat worked, and his eyes teared up again. "A few hours later, a doctor came into the room and told us that one twin had died. Only Devlyn was still with us."

A hushed silence fell over the room. Devlyn fell back in his chair, his eyes wet. "I had a twin?" he croaked.

Vincent nodded. "Delores became hysterical and had to be sedated. Before she fell asleep, she made me swear not to tell anyone what had happened. She felt she wouldn't be able to talk about it, and in her mind, since no one knew to begin with, it was better to erase that baby as if he had never existed. She begged me over and over, and I wanted to do anything to give her peace. So I promised. And I kept that promise until today."

Victor, older by only a couple of years, stared at his brother. "You didn't even tell me," he said slowly.

"No. I knew you would feel obligated to tell Laura, and Laura's compassionate heart would have bled for Delores. So it became our dark secret."

Another of the men spoke up. Pierce identified him most likely as Larkin, Devlyn's younger brother. "So why now? What's going on, Dad?" Suspicion etched his face as if he seldom took things at face value.

Vincent continued in a somber voice. "Yesterday afternoon, I received a phone call from the doctor who was on duty that night. She's well over ninety years old now, and she made a confession to me…a dreadful truth that she has carried with her for all this time."

Pierce tensed as the words sank in. *Gertrude* had called the Wolffs? Stunned, he turned to Nikki. Relief cleansed the dark corners in his heart. She hadn't betrayed him. Fast on the heels of that jubilant realization came intense shame that he had been so quick to accuse her. And grief, because she had faced so much rejection in her life and he had made her live through that hurt again.

Her smile was wry as he stared at her, speechless. He needed to get on his knees and grovel, but the most he could do in that moment was to reach for her hand beneath the table and squeeze it, because the rest of the assemblage was hanging on Vincent's every word.

Bit by bit the old man told his sons and daughter and brother and nephews and all the in-laws the same dreadful tale that Gertrude had shared with Pierce and Nikki. The horrified expressions on the faces of everyone in the room were difficult to watch. Pierce had had a day and a half to process the ugly truth, and he was still having trouble.

One of Victor's sons spoke up. He glanced at Pierce briefly. "I'm Jacob. As a doctor myself, I can hardly fathom what Vincent is telling us."

Pierce felt the urge to explain, to try and stand up for his elderly great-aunt, but Vincent beat him to the punch. He told them about the flu epidemic and why a doctor ended up delivering her niece's child. A niece she had raised as her own daughter. He echoed the old woman's despair when that niece's child died soon after birth.

Vincent was a natural raconteur, and the dark tale unfolded with mesmerizing effect. "Later," he said, "there was an autopsy. The baby had died of a heart defect that was inoperable. It was amazing that he lived even for an hour or two."

Devlyn shook his head, his hands fisted on the table. "He?"

"Yes. The third boy born that night was the one who died. Not your twin."

Pierce tensed. Devlyn stared at him with eyes that held both grief and a dawning astonishment. "So this Pierce fellow…?"

Vincent inclined his head. "He's your brother. He's a Wolff."

Pierce cleared his throat. "My parents don't know the truth. My father is very ill. And the only thing my mother knows is that when I went to be tested as a kidney donor for my father, it was revealed that I am not his son."

"Son of a bitch." Devlyn pounded the table. "That old woman should be hung from the rafters."

Pierce grimaced. "That old woman is part of my family."

"Not really." Devlyn's glare caught Pierce off guard. He'd never thought of it that way—Gertrude wasn't his relative at all.

Nikki put her hand on his leg, under the table where no one could see. Without speaking she telegraphed to him her concern.

Pierce inhaled sharply. "I don't know what I am going to do with this information. My priority right now has to be my parents."

"The people who raised you." Devlyn's rejoinder was sharp.

Surprisingly, Nikki spoke up. "Family is about more than blood," she said softly, though her voice was strong and confident. "Pierce loves his parents very much, so whatever he decides to share with them will have to be honored by all of you. The secret remains in this room until further notice."

Pierce realized that she was speaking now as his lawyer, and the irony of it almost made him smile. She was like a fierce mama bear protecting her cub. "I need some time," he said. "This is a lot to take in. And I found out only today that my father has been matched with a donor and will have surgery next week." He heard Nikki's soft gasp.

Vincent interrupted, his demeanor exhausted. "There's a bit more," he said slowly. "And it affects you all."

A hush fell. The three siblings who were Vincent's offspring looked at him with guarded expressions.

He grimaced. "Delores never recovered from what happened that night. She started drinking, though she quit when she was pregnant with Larkin and then again with Annalise. But her mental state was not good. She had manic periods, and she refused to take any medications, particularly when she found that she could carry other children.

"Though it hurts me to say it, she was never a good mother...not like Victor's dear Laura. Delores blamed Devlyn, I think, for living when her other child died. Irrational, of course, but mental illness is like that. She made an attempt with Larkin and Annalise, but motherhood was too much for her."

He lurched to his feet suddenly, and his whole body shook with violent tremors. "I know my children probably don't believe me, but I never knew the extent of it. I didn't know about the abuse. I swear I would have stopped her. I swear it." He swayed as if he was about to pass out.

Victor rushed to his brother's side. Giving Pierce a look of apology, he said, "He hasn't been well. I need to take him upstairs."

With the older generation gone, there was a moment of stunned silence. This time, it was Devlyn who stood. He walked to where Pierce was sitting and waited. Pierce got to his feet slowly, fully prepared to defend himself physically if necessary.

But in a move that was devastatingly unexpected, Devlyn Wolff grabbed him in a fierce hug and wouldn't let go. Slowly, Pierce's body relaxed. His own eyes damp with unshed tears, he allowed himself to be loved by a man who was his blood brother. Nikki had been right about him connecting to his birth family. He should have listened to her from the start. The sounds of muffled female sobs filled the room. But the tears were cathartic. God only knew where this would lead, but for now, it was enough to be part of the pack.

Nikki felt as if she had been ripped apart and reassembled with some important parts missing. Her chest ached and her eyes were gritty. Pierce seemed wrapped in a fog, and well he should be. It wasn't every day that a man discovered a coterie of relatives, all eager to get to know him.

It was now after nine in the evening, and finally, she and Pierce were tucked away upstairs in an opulent guest suite. They had been given separate rooms, but Pierce had ignored what he'd told Vincent earlier about Nikki being a *friend* and had asked for the more intimate arrangement. Dinner had been served following Vincent's disappearance. During the meal more questions had followed, everyone struggling to understand the entire sequence of what had transpired the night Devlyn and Pierce were born.

Pierce's cousins were as involved as his brothers and sister. Gareth and his wife, Gracie. Jacob, the doctor, and his movie-star spouse, Ariel Dane. And Kieran with his Olivia. Pierce's new sisters-in-law were kind and welcoming, too. Devlyn had married a quiet primary school teacher. Larkin, the closest to being a newlywed, had hitched his star to an heiress with a strong social conscience.

The hardest to read in the whole bunch was the beautiful Annalise, Pierce's sister. She was the only woman who'd grown up in the testosterone-filled Wolff household, and she stared at Pierce as the evening progressed with a look that said she was both shaken and grief-stricken. Her handsome architect husband, Sam, kept an arm around her all night.

But at last the crew took pity on Pierce and let him go for the moment. Daybreak would bring more assimilation, but for now, the enormous house was quiet.

Pierce took his billfold from his pocket and laid it on the dresser. Kicking off his shoes, he stretched and yawned. The commonplace actions restored a sense of balance to the universe.

Finally, he turned and stared at Nikki, his face etched with fatigue. "I don't know how you'll ever forgive me for being such a jackass, but I hope you will. I'm so sorry, Nikki."

She sat on the edge of the king-sized bed and leaned back on her hands. "I could hardly believe me, either. Never in my wildest dreams did I imagine that Gertrude would do what she did."

"I think after we forced the truth from her, she must have been desperate to clean the slate."

"Perhaps." Nikki cocked her head. "How are you feeling?"

He shrugged. "Shell-shocked."

"Any regrets?"

"Tons. Starting with the fact that I was so mean to you." He sat down beside her and took her hand in his, linking their fingers on his thigh. "It's no excuse, I know, but part of the reason I was so angry was that I was scared shitless, if you'll pardon my language. I've never in my life been in such a situation. And honest to God, I didn't know what the right thing to do even was. I'll tell my parents the truth as soon as my dad is stable after the surgery. It won't be easy, but I know I have to."

"Yes," Nikki said quietly, her heart aching for him.

"Truth be told, if you had been the one who spilled the beans, I should have thanked you, because all of this…" He trailed off, his profile pensive as he stared at the floor.

"You're happy and sad and confused and concerned and you haven't a clue how to go forward."

He shot her a grin. "How did you know?"

She leaned her head on his shoulder. "A lucky guess. You're a lucky man."

"I know," he said soberly. Without warning, he moved off the bed onto his knees, this time taking both of her hands in his. He looked up at her, and suddenly it was all there for her to see…his heart, his emotions…wide open.

"I was a bastard, Nicola Parrish," he said, the words gruff and low. His deep-brown eyes were filled with pain and regret. "You deserve a better man. I screwed up the best thing that has ever happened to me. I was so damned determined that I didn't need *anyone,* but God, Nikki, I need *you.* All you ever did was try to help me, and I shoved you away. I'll regret that until the day I die. I am so very, very sorry. If you can find it in your heart to forgive me, I'll spend the rest of my life making it up to you. And since I seem to have an overabundance of family, I'd be honored to share them with you."

Nikki sniffed, refusing to cry anymore. This day had run the gamut, and she was all cried out. Pierce had laid his heart at her feet, and his genuine contrition healed the broken places in her soul. "That's about the nicest offer I've ever received. And I do forgive you, my love."

He sucked in a sharp breath, as if her answer had pulled him off a ledge. "And what if I add a marriage proposal to that? We can figure out the D.C. thing, I swear."

She blinked, her heart beginning to thud slow and hard. "You're overwrought," she said. "Don't do anything rash. And besides, I already told them I'm not coming."

"My God," he said hoarsely. "Why?"

"I couldn't leave you," she simply. "I didn't want to."

He paled. "So you were willing to take a chance on me, and then I tossed you aside?"

"Don't beat yourself up. It wasn't all about you. I decided I wasn't cut out for high-stakes legal practice in the seat of politics. Though it *was* flattering to be asked."

He bent his head and exhaled audibly before lifting his chin and meeting her eyes with his. "I love you." He said it simply. Fervently. As though he'd been waiting forever to speak those three syllables in just that way.

"You do?"

He nodded, smiling. "And you love me, too. Why else would you have showed up today and walked with me into the lion's den?"

Freeing her hands, she ruffled his hair. "Prurient curiosity? Billable hours?"

He tugged her arm, tumbling her off balance until she landed on the soft carpet beside him. Leaning over her, he cupped her breast, stroking it until she felt her belly curl in pleasure.

They were both fully clothed. But suddenly the room felt too hot for anything but bare skin. She licked her lips. "Shouldn't we get undressed?" Her heart pounded in her throat and her mouth was dry as cotton.

"Maybe later." He grinned wolfishly, rebounding with impressive speed from his exhaustion. Shoving her skirt to her waist, he unzipped his pants and settled between her legs. But his face fell as he realized he had no protection. He groaned, his erection nudging urgently at her belly.

"Unbelievable. I propose to a woman and I can't even seal the deal."

Nikki giggled, reaching into the side-seam pocket of her dress. "Lucky for you, I'm a planner." She extracted two condoms and laughed out loud at the look of bemusement on his face.

"Thank God for that. I'll never complain about your OCD ways again." Sheathing himself quickly, he returned to the spot where they had left off.

When he entered her slowly, her breath caught. "I do love you, Pierce. I should have said it before."

"You're a cautious woman. Nothing wrong with that." He rolled to his back, taking her with him, settling her legs on either side of his hips. The new position hit nerve centers she never knew she had.

She braced her hands on his chest, already feeling the first ripples of an intense orgasm. When he grabbed her hips and thrust wildly, they both toppled over the edge in unison, their cries mingling as their bodies clung to the last vestiges of release.

She slumped on top of him, boneless, spent, so incredibly dazed with happiness. She thought Pierce had fallen asleep until she felt words rumble from his throat.

"I never imagined I'd fall for a lawyer."

She shivered as her skin cooled and the night waned. "Well, I guess that's okay, 'cause I never thought I'd fall for a millionaire."

He pinched her butt. "That's *billionaire*," he said with a teasing grin. "And as soon as I can manage it, I'll put a tastelessly large diamond on your finger to prove it."

She kissed his throat, loving the way he groaned when she raked him with her teeth. "The zeroes aren't important. All I need is you."

"I guess that makes us a family, then." He kissed her

nose. "And just so you know, I'm going to want to see those hot-pink high heels you told me about…in the very near future."

"Just the shoes?" He was hard again. She moved restlessly, wondering if she could reach the last condom.

He left her long enough to do what needed to be done, and then lifted her onto the bed, moving over her and into her with intent. "We'll start with the shoes, my dear lady lawyer. And I'll negotiate the rest."

"I don't come cheap," she warned. "You hired the best."

"Worth every penny," he said, groaning as he reached the end. "I'll never want anyone the way I want you."

Nikki closed her eyes, smiling. It was all she could ask for…and so much more.…

Epilogue

Nikki unfastened the seat belt that had been digging into her rounded stomach and stepped out of the car with Pierce's help. As she stretched and winced, Wolff Castle loomed in front of her, its stately facade now familiar and dear.

She leaned her head on her husband's arm. "Seems awfully quiet. I thought everyone was coming for dinner."

"They are," Pierce said. "Maybe they're all upstairs changing clothes."

The baby girl in her womb gave a firm kick, stealing Nikki's breath for a moment. "I can't believe Annalise won the bet about the sex and the confirmed due date. Everyone else thought it was a boy for sure. Are you sorry?" she asked, looking up at him with faint anxiety. They'd had their ultrasound only that morning, and he had cried along with her when the doctor told them the news. Even still… the Wolffs were a masculine lot.

Pierce took her face in his hands and kissed her gently. "I am beyond thrilled," he said. "Don't be a goose. Nothing is more precious than a baby dressed all in pink. She'll be as beautiful and smart as her mama."

Hand in hand, they entered the house and headed for the formal salon, Pierce leading the way. In the alcove outside the door, Nikki held back. "Can we stop by the kitchen? Dinner is a long way off and I'm hungry."

"Again?" The teasing glint in his eyes told her he wasn't serious.

"Watch it, wise guy. It's not smart to mess with a pregnant lady."

"We'll grab something in a minute," he said. "Let's see if any of the others are around."

He opened the door, and as Nikki stepped forward, a huge unison roar greeted them. "Congratulations!"

Nikki blinked, tears welling in her eyes as they so often did now. The entire Wolff family filled the room, along with Pierce's parents, Mr. and Mrs. Avery. Pink bows, floral swags and balloons festooned the walls. A cherry drop-leaf table groaned beneath the weight of a mountain of baby gifts. A second table held a silver punch bowl and a small version of a wedding cake, this one topped with a pair of pink satin booties.

Nikki sniffed. "I don't know what to say."

Annalise stepped forward, her face beaming. "We wanted to be your first baby shower. Daddy insisted we buy everything in both pink and blue since we wouldn't know until today, so upstairs is a pile of stuff we'll be donating to charity."

Everyone broke into laughter, and soon Nikki and Pierce were seated front and center so the unwrapping could begin. Car seats. A stroller. More beautiful clothes than a baby could possibly wear in a month. Practical items, whimsical stuffed toys, everything a new mom and dad could need.

When the last box was emptied, Vincent Wolff stepped forward, handing Nikki a long, slender box that looked as if it might contain a man's necktie. Curious, she smiled at Pierce as she opened it.

Together, they lifted the sheaf of papers inside. Nikki's lower lip wobbled. It was the deed to a plot of land on Wolff Mountain.

Vincent waved a hand, not able to meet their eyes as he walked back to his seat. "Build a vacation home, whatever you want." Then he looked at the Averys solemnly. "And I've something for you as well, if you'll step into my study afterward. To thank you for raising such a fine man, our son."

Nikki felt Pierce's tension and shivered when he stood. The whole room fell silent. Slowly, he approached his biological father, bent and hugged him. "Thank you, *Father*. This means a lot to us."

Seconds later, chatter erupted, dissolving the moment of intense emotion. Pierce was pulled away to help his brothers assemble a tricycle that wouldn't be needed for months and months. The women began serving food.

Nikki looked around the room, marveling at the changes in her life. For the first time, she had a family of her own. She, Pierce and their baby girl. But even as the thought crossed her mind, she realized it wasn't entirely true. The amazing fact was, she had gone from having *no* family to having *three*. Because the Wolffs and the Averys had made her one of their own.

Her world had come full circle. Complete. As unending as the platinum wedding band she wore. And love had made it so....

* * * * *

If you loved Pierce's story, don't miss a single novel in
THE MEN OF WOLFF MOUNTAIN,
a series from
USA TODAY *bestselling author Janice Maynard:*

INTO HIS PRIVATE DOMAIN
A TOUCH OF PERSUASION
IMPOSSIBLE TO RESIST
THE MAID'S DAUGHTER
ALL GROWN UP
TAMING THE LONE WOLFF

All available now from Harlequin Desire!

COMING NEXT MONTH FROM

◆ HARLEQUIN®

Desire

Available November 5, 2013

#2263 THE SECRET HEIR OF SUNSET RANCH
The Slades of Sunset Ranch • by Charlene Sands
Rancher Justin Slade returns from war a hero...and finds out he's a father.
But as things with his former fling heat back up, he must keep their child's
paternity secret—someone's life depends on it.

#2264 TO TAME A COWBOY
Texas Cattleman's Club: The Missing Mogul
by Jules Bennett
When rodeo star Ryan Grant decides to hang up his spurs and settle down,
he resolves to wrangle the heart of his childhood friend. But will she let
herself be caught by this untamable cowboy?

#2265 CLAIMING HIS OWN
Billionaires and Babies • by Olivia Gates
Russian tycoon Maksim refuses to become like his abusive father, so he
leaves the woman he loves and their son. But now he's returned a changed
man...ready to stake his claim.

#2266 ONE TEXAS NIGHT...
Lone Star Legacy • by Sara Orwig
After a forbidden night of passion with his best friend's sister, Jared Weston
gets a second chance. But can this risk taker convince the cautious Allison
to risk it all on him?

#2267 EXPECTING A BOLTON BABY
The Bolton Brothers • by Sarah M. Anderson
One night with his investor's daughter shouldn't have led to more, but
when she announces she's pregnant, real estate mogul Bobby Bolton must
decide what's more important—family or money.

#2268 THE PREGNANCY PLOT
by Paula Roe
AJ wants a baby, and her ex is the perfect donor. But their simple baby plan
turns complicated when Matt decides he wants a second chance with the
one who got away!

———————

**YOU CAN FIND MORE INFORMATION ON UPCOMING HARLEQUIN® TITLES,
FREE EXCERPTS AND MORE AT WWW.HARLEQUIN.COM.**

HDCNM1013

REQUEST YOUR FREE BOOKS!
2 FREE NOVELS PLUS 2 FREE GIFTS!

✦ HARLEQUIN®

Desire

ALWAYS POWERFUL, PASSIONATE AND PROVOCATIVE

YES! Please send me 2 FREE Harlequin Desire® novels and my 2 FREE gifts (gifts are worth about $10). After receiving them, if I don't wish to receive any more books, I can return the shipping statement marked "cancel." If I don't cancel, I will receive 6 brand-new novels every month and be billed just $4.55 per book in the U.S. or $4.99 per book in Canada. That's a savings of at least 13% off the cover price! It's quite a bargain! Shipping and handling is just 50¢ per book in the U.S. and 75¢ per book in Canada.* I understand that accepting the 2 free books and gifts places me under no obligation to buy anything. I can always return a shipment and cancel at any time. Even if I never buy another book, the two free books and gifts are mine to keep forever.

225/326 HDN F4ZC

Name	(PLEASE PRINT)	
Address		Apt. #
City	State/Prov.	Zip/Postal Code

Signature (if under 18, a parent or guardian must sign)

Mail to the **Harlequin® Reader Service:**

IN U.S.A.: P.O. Box 1867, Buffalo, NY 14240-1867
IN CANADA: P.O. Box 609, Fort Erie, Ontario L2A 5X3

Want to try two free books from another line?
Call 1-800-873-8635 or visit www.ReaderService.com.

* Terms and prices subject to change without notice. Prices do not include applicable taxes. Sales tax applicable in N.Y. Canadian residents will be charged applicable taxes. Offer not valid in Quebec. This offer is limited to one order per household. Not valid for current subscribers to Harlequin Desire books. All orders subject to credit approval. Credit or debit balances in a customer's account(s) may be offset by any other outstanding balance owed by or to the customer. Please allow 4 to 6 weeks for delivery. Offer available while quantities last.

Your Privacy—The Harlequin® Reader Service is committed to protecting your privacy. Our Privacy Policy is available online at www.ReaderService.com or upon request from the Harlequin Reader Service.

We make a portion of our mailing list available to reputable third parties that offer products we believe may interest you. If you prefer that we not exchange your name with third parties, or if you wish to clarify or modify your communication preferences, please visit us at www.ReaderService.com/consumerschoice or write to us at Harlequin Reader Service Preference Service, P.O. Box 9062, Buffalo, NY 14269. Include your complete name and address.

HD13R

SPECIAL EXCERPT FROM

HARLEQUIN®

Desire

Harlequin® Desire presents

THE SECRET HEIR OF SUNSET RANCH,

part of

USA TODAY *bestselling author*

Charlene Sands's
miniseries

THE SLADES OF SUNSET RANCH

Returning from the front lines, rancher Justin Slade is about to get the surprise of his life…

She was a stunner.

He remembered those deep jade eyes, that pouty mouth and the Marilyn Monroe hair only a few women could pull off. He would've bet his last dollar that he'd never see her again. And now here she was…in the flesh.

Maybe he was wrong. Maybe she only looked like the woman he'd met in New York City that one weekend a year and a half ago.

Justin removed his Stetson and her eyes flickered.

"B-Brett? Is that really you?" The hope in her voice confused him. "I don't understand. We were told you were killed in a gun battle."

Silently, he cursed the bet he'd made with Brett Applegate during a weekend leave in New York before they headed back to their forward operating base in Afghanistan.

The price of the bet? Reversing roles for the weekend.

They'd emptied the contents of their pockets. Good ole Brett had scooped up all seven hundred-dollar bills Justin had dumped onto the bunk. "Gonna have me some fun being you," he'd said, grinning like a fool.

Justin had blown Brett's meager cash on a bottle of house wine at the hotel, and afterward she'd taken him to her tiny fourth-floor walk-up. He'd been looking for a good time and they'd clicked.

"I'm not Brett Applegate," he told the blonde.

She studied him. "But I remember you. Don't you remember me? I'm Kat Grady."

"I remember you, *sugar*." But he didn't have a clue why Kat was here, looking gorgeous, in front of the Applegate home.

Her eyes softened. "No one else has ever called me that."

Justin winced at her sweet tone. "My name isn't Brett. I'm Justin Slade and I live about twenty miles north of here. Brett and I served together on a tour of duty in the marines."

Her voice dropped off. "You're Justin…*Slade?*"

He nodded.

"*Sunset Ranch* Justin Slade?"

He nodded again. "Maybe we should go inside the house and talk. I'll try to explain."

But Kat has a bombshell secret of her own.
Find out more in
THE SECRET HEIR OF SUNSET RANCH
Available November 2013 from Harlequin Desire.

Copyright © 2013 by Charlene Swink

HARLEQUIN®

Desire

ALWAYS POWERFUL, PASSIONATE AND PROVOCATIVE.

When rodeo star Ryan Grant decides to hang up his spurs and settle down, he resolves to wrangle the heart of his childhood friend. But will she let herself be caught by this untamable cowboy?

Look for *TO TAME A COWBOY* by Jules Bennett, the next title in the *Texas Cattleman's Club: The Missing Mogul* miniseries, next month.

Don't miss a single story from this miniseries! Available now from Harlequin Desire.

Wherever books and ebooks are sold.

RUMOR HAS IT
by Maureen Child

DEEP IN A TEXAN'S HEART
by Sara Orwig

SOMETHING ABOUT THE BOSS...
by Yvonne Lindsay

THE LONE STAR CINDERELLA
by Maureen Child

—— www.Harlequin.com ——

HD73277